SKIN DEEP

ALSO BY HUGH MILLER

An Echo of Justice
Home Ground
Snow on the Wind
The District Nurse
The Rejuvenators
The Dissector
Ambulance

SKIN DEEP

Hugh Miller

St. Martin's Press

New York

Library of Congress Cataloging-in-Publication Data

Miller, Hugh
    Skin deep / Hugh Miller.
      p. cm.
    ISBN 0-312-08293-2
    I. Title.
   PR6063.I373s55   1992
    823'.914—dc20   92-20967
                                                      CIP

First published in Great Britain by Victor Gollancz Ltd.

First U.S. Edition: September 1992

10 9 8 7 6 5 4 3 2 1

SKIN DEEP

Outside beyond the thick drapes he heard thunder rattle, like the clearing of a vast throat. The notion amused him. He yawned and stretched out his legs. It must be very late now. He saw his own brown hand on the arm of the easy chair, blue smoke curling from the smouldering joint pinched between his finger and thumb. The journey his eyes made from one hand to the other took a long time. He stared at the glass he held and felt himself smile.

All this was a bonus, it was not what he had come for. He had expected the visit to be brief, the atmosphere brisk, businesslike. But he had been allowed to sit in peace among this luxury for a long time. He had been given hashish to smoke and rum to drink and there was no sign, yet, that they would finally get down to business.

He inhaled sharply on the joint, trying to remember his name. He was . . . It wouldn't come. That happened often when he smoked hash. He forget his alias. There had been so many.

'Kewal,' he murmured, making his host turn from whatever he was doing at the table.

He hadn't the energy to explain. Kewal was the only name he could remember. It was his real name, the first one he had ever possessed. Kewal Majumdar. He had been very young the last time anyone called him that.

He swallowed a mouthful of rum, the best he had ever tasted. It didn't burn, no matter how much of it he gulped, or how fast. It was like drinking dark silk.

He looked round the room, his head seeming to turn on a geared mount that could not be hurried. Where was his friend? Where was . . . He couldn't remember the name. There was no sign of him. Only the host, coming across the room again with the rum bottle. Kewal smiled as his glass was topped up.

Another drag on the joint, letting the smoke out slowly, then a deep swallow from the glass, and he felt the well-being slip away. A pain, heavy as a dread, rolled across his chest. He sat forward in the chair, gasping.

He had been stoned before, often, stoned *and* drunk at the same time. He had never felt like this. With a huge effort he pushed himself to his feet, vaguely aware that he had dropped the glass on the carpet.

His throat was expanding. He could feel his heart flutter against his ribs. When he tried to swallow and clear the sensation of fullness at the back of his tongue he found the muscles no longer responded. His heart banged harder, its beat slowing. He touched his face with a heavy hand and felt cold slippery sweat.

The host was standing in front of him, staring and half smiling, attentive as a waiter. He was uncoiling a length of cord between his hands.

'Kewal . . . '

The sound was dusty dry, a croak, but he said it again, his name, the real one. If he held on to it he would have control of himself. All he had to do was keep saying Kewal, over and over.

But when he tried a third time he could not remember it, and his voice refused to work, anyway.

He began to fall. There was no power to make his hands come up to break the impact. His chest, then his face, slammed on to the carpet. He heard his heart, frighteningly loud, and felt himself being rolled on to his back. He looked up at the host and tried to plead to be lifted. No sound came from him but the smallest gasp, then he knew, in a jolt of clarity, that he was going to die.

ONE

Mike Fletcher came into the bedroom, dum-de-dumming the refrain of a song they had played before the eight o'clock news. He carried a tray with two brimming mugs of tea and a plateful of buttered toast between them.

'Breakfast.'

He put the tray on the dressing table beside Kate Barbour and stood back, watching her. She was hunched forward on the stool, a towel across the shoulders of her jacket, brushing her auburn hair with short agitated strokes.

'I'm late,' she said, glaring at her reflection. 'I didn't look at the clock until a couple of minutes ago.'

'You're no later than usual.' Mike picked up his mug and took a gulp. 'When I brought the tea yesterday you were still clambering into your tights.'

'I've an early clinic. I wanted time to go over the notes on the first case. Now I'll have to busk it. If I don't, I'll be behind all morning.' Her eyes in the mirror switched to his. 'Will you be free for lunch?'

'Well . . . I'm not sure.'

'I'll buy.'

Mike made an effort not to look reluctant.

'A lot'll depend on what's come in overnight. Friday can be a tricky day.'

'We should talk,' Kate said. 'And we shouldn't leave it too long.'

'I'll ring you,' he promised. 'No later than eleven.'

He snatched up a triangle of toast and wandered to the

9

window. It was raining again, big windblown drops starbursting on the glass. Against the darkness of swinging branches he saw his own mirrored face, absently chewing. Forty-four next month, he thought. A mature operator with more experience than most. He had even been called an investigative frontrunner. When it came to relationships, though, he could still walk into the blades like a dumb kid.

'You haven't forgotten what we were talking about last night?' Kate turned, a lipstick held to her mouth. 'I know you were whacked, but — '

'I remember.'

Last night at dinner — a celebration, the second anniversary of their first dinner together — he drank probably three brandies too many. Consequently he became receptive to ideas he would normally resist. He remembered the gentle thrust of Kate's argument and the numb immobility where his parry should have been. Later, back here at her place with more brandies, an agreement had *nearly* been reached when Mike suddenly declared he could no longer think straight and would have to go to bed.

'Make the effort today,' Kate said, capping the lipstick and standing up. 'I'm sure a man in your position's got the clout to delegate if he needs to. We can have a nice lunch at Alexiou's and round off our little agenda while we're at it. I hate leaving important issues dangling.'

Mike didn't fail to notice he had been patronised and bulldozed at one swipe. Through a mouthful of toast he promised again to call. Kate took a sip of tea, looked at the clock and said she had to run. At the front door she kissed Mike's cheek and reminded him to drop the catch when he left.

He watched from the kitchen window as she clopped down the path, magnificently decisive in her high heels and flapping trenchcoat. Why didn't an animating sight like that warm him? How could he feel invaded by someone closer than his own sweat?

He turned and saw his weary face again in the mirror above the sink. Tired or freshly charged he always looked the same, an incipient mandarin. He combed his fingers through lawless hair and jumped as his pager bleeped.

At the telephone in the hall he tapped in the station number and waited. Sergeant Brewster answered.

'This is DI Fletcher. My device just squeaked.'

The sergeant asked him to wait. He was back in seconds.

'Sounds like a murder,' he said. 'Waste ground down at Kelso's Wharf, where the little factories dump their rubbish. Male Asian half buried in the tip. The body was spotted by school kids on a passing train. That's all I have. DC Chinnery posted the message. He says he'll meet you there.'

Mike went back to the kitchen and put on the kettle. There was time for another cup of tea, or two if he wanted. It would be a while yet before they moved the body, what with forensic crawling over everything with their cameras and brushes and vacuum cleaners.

He brought the tray with Kate's mug and the rest of the toast to the kitchen table. He emptied the mug into the sink and put it in the basin.

'Bags of time,' he muttered, topping up his mug from the teapot.

He sat down at the table and sighed. It was nice, for once, not to rush. He had time for more tea, time to finish the toast, time to let Kate get to the hospital so he could call her and say how sorry he was about lunch.

TWO

Spectators were bunched at the steel-barred gates, craning and tiptoeing, a couple of them perched on the gateposts. All they could see was a high canvas windbreak, gatelegged around a point on the wharf twenty feet from the river. Even so they watched, muttering to each other without taking their eyes off the expanse of grey canvas.

'Garrett's here,' a man told his neighbour, whose face was pushed against the bars. 'I heard one of the cops telling his mate.'

'Garrett?'

'The pathologist. The one the papers christened the Death Doctor. He was in all the headlines when that solicitor butchered his wife and kids.'

'Oh. Him.'

'A brilliant bod, by all accounts.'

'I suppose so.' The neighbour blinked at the windbreak for a minute. 'It's a funny way to make a living. Nine to five, cutting up dead people.'

'Well, if you look at it that way . . .'

'It's the *only* way to look at it. It's what he does, isn't it? That's a pathologist's job.'

'True,' the first man conceded. 'A ghoulish line of business, when you view it cold. You'd need to be a bit twisted to want to do it in the first place, I suppose.'

'Twisted? Fucking bent, more like.'

Beyond the windbreak policemen and technicians worked systematically, expressionless with cold and tedium, performing their parts in the forensic routine. Near the rubbish tip Detective Constable Chinnery stood taking notes. Dr Garrett stood beside him, a tubby little man in a heavy tweed coat with a blue scarf half obscuring his mouth.

'Thank heaven for mechanical memory,' he said, hefting a micro recorder in his palm. He put it to his mouth, pressed a button and spoke to it.

'Testing, one, two, three . . .'

He rewound, listened to the toytown replica of his voice, ran it back again, switched on and began his preliminary description of the dead man.

'The body is positioned upside down, the legs bent and embedded knee-deep a third of the way up a twenty-foot pile of decaying commercial waste.'

The deceased was obviously an Asian. In death the skin of his face had lost its rich umber; it was dun coloured now and smeared with green slime from the tip. The blood-rimmed right eye was open, the left one was gone. The tongue, dark blue and swollen, protruded startlingly between the teeth. Around the neck a cord was tied so tightly it disappeared for most of its length into a deep groove in the skin. An identical cord bound the hands at the back.

'Superficial signs indicate traumatic asphyxia. A conjunctival haemorrhage has bulged through the eyelid of the intact eye. There are petechial haemorrhages on the eyelids, also on both cheeks and around the mouth.'

Garrett switched off the recorder. He turned to DC Chinnery, who was making a note of the dead man's clothes.

'He'd be about the same age as yourself, I'd say. Late twenties, early thirties.'

'He looks older,' Chinnery said.

'The missing eye does that. Imagine him with sunglasses on. That's a young face. Too young to be dead.'

'He must have gone through hell.'

'Well . . .'

'Would you say this is a classic sadistic killing, sir?'

A weakness of young Chinnery's, Garrett had noticed, was

that he required people and events to fit categories. He longed for a tidier world than the chaotic structure of life would ever permit.

'In this job it doesn't do to call anything classic,' Garrett said. 'I'll say something's standard, or typical, or even archetypal, but classic's not a word to use in forensic work. It implies excellence. There's nothing excellent about crime.'

'A *typical* sadistic killing, then?'

'No.' Dr Garrett pushed his gold-rimmed glasses up on his nose. 'It's a fairly unusual attempt to make the killing appear sadistic — the bound hands, the gouged-out eye. But the man was dead before those things were done to him.'

Chinnery seemed disappointed.

'Look at the neck and face,' Garrett said. 'Lots of pinpoint haemorrhaging and bruising, signs that the victim was alive when the ligature was put round his neck. But the eye socket, see . . .' He leaned forward and touched the edge of the dark hole with his pencil. 'Avascular tissue. No sign of bleeding, no clots. And the wrists. Bound as tight as can be, but there's not a trace of a bruise. Dead men don't bruise. They don't bleed either. Ergo, this man was dead before he was bound and mutilated.'

Albert Coker, taciturn and chronically asthmatic, came wheezing from Dr Garrett's car where the pathology workbag lay open on the bonnet. He eased past DC Chinnery and stood in front of the body. From a thick roll he tore off a plastic bag and put it carefully over the dead man's head, trapping dirt and debris and such clues as might be there.

'Put one over the hands as well,' Dr Garrett said.

'I was going to,' Albert snapped. 'The feet too, when they're dug out.'

Albert was a few months off his fortieth year as an attendant at the city mortuary. He often assisted Dr Garrett at the scenes of serious crimes and by now he knew the procedures better than most people.

'I'm sure he finds me a terrible pain in the bum,' Garrett muttered to Chinnery. 'When I'm not interfering I'm getting in his way.'

Mike Fletcher came across the wharf, skirting a throng of technicians. He nodded to Dr Garrett and winked at Chinnery. For a moment he stared at the body. With the bag over the head it looked more grotesque than before.

'What's the story?'

'Sketchy at the moment,' Chinnery said. 'Asian male, thirtyish, no identification. He was apparently strangled with a cord, mutilated, then dumped here some time during the past twelve hours.'

Mike nodded, as if he had expected to hear nothing different.

'On the way here,' he said, 'I was thinking about a pending file at the station, one we opened a week or two back.'

'Which one's that, sir?'

'Half a dozen letters — one sent to the Chief Constable, one to a newspaper, some to leaders in the Asian community. All delivered over a three-day period.'

'Threatening letters, you mean?' Dr Garrett said.

Mike nodded.

'We get a lot handed in during the year. Mostly they go into pending files because there's no thread to follow and the case usually dries up, anyway. But this last lot were stronger than most. Direct death threats, aimed specifically at Asians.'

'You reckon this is connected?' Chinnery said.

'I can't help wondering.' Mike turned to Dr Garrett. 'Was he hanged, by any chance?'

'No. Why do you ask?'

'A couple of the letters mentioned stringing-up.'

'It could be careless terminology, if there is a connection,' Garrett said. 'Or thwarted intent — you need help to hang somebody. This man definitely wasn't hanged.'

'You can be certain of that?'

'As certain as I can be of anything. When a person is hanged he doesn't choke to death. He dies almost instantaneously from cardiac failure, caused by the impact of the rope on the carotid vessels. Also, there's never any purpling, no congestion or haemorrhages, no signs at all of choking. The face is invariably pale and unmarked. And besides that, in this case the imprint of the ligature is too low for hanging — and there's no displacement of the cervical vertebrae.'

'I'm always learning,' Mike said.

They watched as Albert Coker and three technicians eased the body away from the rubbish tip. The moment the lower legs came free it was obvious they were broken.

'Put him on the ground,' Dr Garrett said.

He crouched by the body and drew up the sopping trouser legs, exposing mangled skin and protruding ends of fractured bone. The examination took less than a minute. Garrett stood up again, grunting with the effort.

'A hammer job,' he said, 'done after he was dead.'

When Albert Coker had covered the feet with plastic bags the corpse was bagged, put in the back of a black van and driven out past the crowd at the gates.

With the departure of the victim, the investigation began to diffuse. Technicians went back to their labs to examine the evidence they had gathered; policemen set off to knock on doors. Mike Fletcher told DC Chinnery to circulate the dead man's description and check the missing-person records.

'And while you're doing that I'll have another look at that pending file.' Mike turned to Dr Garrett. 'Can I come over to the mortuary later for a summary of your verdict?'

'Of course. Could you leave it until after six?'

'If you want.'

'I've been given a bottle of malt, you see. It's a new one to me — I'm sure you'd like to be at the grand opening.'

'You have a fine and generous heart,' Mike said.

'Yes, I believe I'm known for it.'

'How come you're waiting till after six before you have a tot?'

'My wife, with the connivance of a cardiologist who's miles too smart for his own good, got me to promise I'll never again touch alcohol before evening.'

'I'll be there at one minute past six,' Mike said.

THREE

Tall and straight-backed, heavier than he wished to be but lean-looking nevertheless, Detective Chief Superintendent Derek Bingham believed himself hindered by the fact that his age didn't show.

He was easy to like on sight. He had round, handsomely lopsided features, wiry brown hair and lively grey-green eyes. There was a spring of athletic health in his step; the general impression of vigorous youth was reinforced by the way he dressed — loose, fashionable clothes, always bordering on the casual.

At a glance most people would say Bingham was in his thirties. Longer inspection would narrow that down: thirty-four, thirty-five. In fact he was forty-eight. Thirty years in the police and twenty-six years of wedded fidelity to the same woman should, he believed, have aged him cruelly. But in fact, because he looked so fresh-faced and artlessly boyish, he often had to strive for the measure of authority his rank would have guaranteed, if he'd looked his years.

At 11.15 a.m., walking stealthily, he entered the CID room and looked around. Only Mike Fletcher was there, at his desk with his back to the door. Bingham crept up behind him and slapped a hand on his shoulder.

'Michael! My secretary says you were looking for me.'

Mike sat back, clutching his pounding heart.

'Jesus,' he breathed. 'That was close.'

Bingham came round to the front of the desk and sat down.

'You can see where my skill lies,' he said darkly. 'Any witless bugger can frighten a man to death. But to *nearly* snuff him. Well. We're talking talent.' He folded his arms. 'What do you want?'

'I thought I should fill you in on the murder enquiry. And get your opinion on something.'

Bingham nodded, smothering a yawn.

'Don't take that personally,' he said. 'It's been a tedious morning so far. I've spent an hour and a half with the watch committee. They're an uncommonly tense bunch, don't you think?'

'It's righteous rigidity,' Mike said. 'A prerequisite for the job.' He picked up a letter from the file in front of him and passed it across. 'Do you remember this?'

Bingham looked at it.

'Yes. Crank circular. One of several.'

'The dead man found at Kelso's Wharf this morning was an Asian. He hadn't been strung up, like the letter says, but he'd been strangled and mutilated.'

'And you want to know if I think there could be a connection?'

'I want to know if you think we've grounds for assuming the *likelihood* of a connection.'

Bingham crossed his legs and thought about it.

'Let's see the other letters.'

The uniform layout showed they were all from the same source. The style of the text was unvarying from letter to letter: its keynote was stiff outrage.

'"How *can* the civic authorities permit these people to colonise our community the way they do?"' Bingham read aloud, trying for a breathless-blimp voice. '"They bring with them their diseases, their primitive domestic customs and their propensity for social subversion. How *can* they be allowed to buy into our business communities, unresisted? By what right do they expand like malignancies until their cartels and price-cutting gain them a stranglehold on entire commercial sectors?"'

18

'I hear the essence of that in the canteen all the time,' Mike said. 'Everyday racist bullshit.'

'But you think this is different?'

'The last bit is.'

Bingham turned over the letter and looked at the final paragraph. He cleared his throat and read again:

'"If the police and the council between them don't take official steps to curb the spread of Asian commercial influence, if they take no action to stem the tide of social and racial catastrophe, then unofficial steps will be taken. Asians will die. They will be strung up for their iniquities, they will be sent to their deaths torn and broken, knowing their transgressions have bought them a calibre of justice reserved for those who invade the domain of their natural superiors."'

Bingham leafed through the other letters again, reading snatches. Finally he put them all back on the desk and looked at Mike.

'How did the man die?'

Mike told him the ligature had probably caused death. He described the injuries that were inflicted later.

'Do we know who he is?'

'Jishrah Gopal, a warehouseman,' Mike said. 'He was identified an hour ago — his boss recognised him from the description we circulated. Jishrah was thirty-two and single. He lived alone, so far as we know. A forensic team and two of our lads are going over his bedsit right now. We should have Dr Garrett's report some time this evening.' Mike drummed his fingers. 'What do you think? Do we assume a likely connection between the threat letters and this murder?'

Bingham stared at his knees for a minute.

'Yes,' he said at last. 'As long as you remember your likelihood is an outsider. So far, anyway. We have letters threatening that Asians will die, and an Asian is now dead, clearly murdered. So we've either got a coincidence or a fulfilled threat. Coincidence is the stronger likelihood at present, but the minor one can't be disregarded.'

Mike took a one-page forensic report from the flap pocket of the file and read it.

'There's nothing materially substantial to go on with the letters,' he said. 'The paper's mass produced, available at dozens of local outlets. The typewriter's a portable with idiosyncrasies — a wonky capital T for one — but it's a very popular Japanese model, there must be hundreds of them in the city.'

'So although the letters can be cautiously regarded as evidence, they aren't much help?'

'Well, they might be, sir. I think if we asked around, and if we really got lucky, we could find the writer.'

Bingham looked politely sceptical.

'The style of the letters,' Mike said, 'it's very, ah, expository. It's tub-thumping stuff. Characters who express themselves like that don't restrict it to letters. They shoot off their faces. The language of these letters is very much a tone of voice — it could be a hard slog tracking it down, but I'm pretty sure somebody will recognise it.'

'I'm moved by your faith,' Bingham said. 'It'll be a hell of a slog, as you say, and I'll tell you now there won't be extra manpower available. But there are no good reasons why life should be easy for coppers.' He stood up. 'Keep me posted. The race angle could have this thing blowing up in our faces if we don't get a quick result.' He went to the door and paused. 'One other thing for you to think about,' he said.

'Sir?'

'Why do women yawn as soon as they wake up in the morning?'

'Offhand, I've no idea.'

'Ponder, then.'

At the mortuary Dr Garrett ushered Mike into the office and closed the door. With some ceremony he took the new bottle of malt whisky from his briefcase and half filled two miniature lab beakers. He handed one to Mike and told him to take a chair.

'Whisky should always be savoured in a sitting position,' he said, sinking into the old swivel by the desk. 'Your good health, Michael.'

'And yours.'

They sipped carefully, watching each other.

'Very much like Glenmorangie,' Dr Garrett said after a minute. 'The same tang, the soft bite on the throat . . . '

'Or a velvety version of Old Parr . . . '

'Yes, yes, there's that, too.'

They issued a few more vague evaluations, sipping and clucking their way to the bottom of the beakers. Then they had second measures for the sheer pleasure of drinking malt. Halfway down, Mike turned businesslike and asked about the autopsy on Jishrah Gopal.

'He died about a week ago,' Dr Garrett said, 'going by the discoloration over the right iliac fossa, and one or two other signs. The body was probably kept indoors until some time yesterday.'

'And he died of strangulation?'

'Yes, he did. But there was something unusual.' Garrett paused to swallow more whisky. 'I took samples of blood, as I routinely do, and the lab actually telephoned the results to me a few minutes ago — in view of the unexpected finding, you understand.'

'And what was that?'

'A drug was present. Haloperidol. It's a psychotrophic agent, not related to the promazine group, but it has much the same ataraxic properties — '

'You lost me at psychotrophic.'

'I'm sorry. It's a powerful suppressor, shall we say. They use it a lot in the treatment of psychotic disorders. Your lady could tell you all about it.'

'Was there a lot of it in Gopal's blood?'

'A great deal. Enough to make him very woozy and disorientated. A minute or so after it was administered, I doubt he would have been able to stand.'

'Was he drugged long before he was strangled?'

'A few minutes, probably, the degree of absorption into the blood indicates as much. By the time it came to the murder, I don't think he would have known what was happening to him.'

'So the sequence of events was doping, strangulation, mutilation.'

'Correct.'

'Crazy,' Mike said. 'We find what looks like a barbarous murder, then it turns out the killer made sure the victim hardly suffered at all.'

'Indeed,' Garrett said. 'Criminal motives are getting beyond my grasp. Maybe it's a good thing I'm retiring in a couple of years.'

Mike emptied his glass and put it on the desk.

'I won't strain my head much until we know more about Jishrah Gopal. After you've offered me a parting glass, and when I've graciously accepted and sunk it, I'm going back to the office to write up what I've got so far. That's the first scenario. The second one is, I go home to my own quiet apartment and turn in early. Number three is me facing the music round at Kate's house.'

'I thought things were going smoothly in that area of your life.'

'Blandly,' Mike said, 'that's how things were going. No issues were being confronted. The relationship's engine was in neutral. Then last night we had a celebration dinner, and I had a few too many and started making commitments.'

'To what?'

'To change. I halfway agreed to move in with Kate. For good, instead of on and off like I do now. The idea, put simply, is for me to sell my own place and take on the house fifty-fifty with her.'

'You agreed to that?'

'I *suggested* it, God help me.'

'Lord.'

'Drink,' Mike said. 'Blame drink.' He held out his glass. Dr Garrett uncapped the whisky bottle. 'In cold daylight I know I can't go through with it. I've got to tell Kate that.'

'The sooner the better, then.'

22

'Sure. And this is just the stuff to give me the guts. But if I have much more of it before I go round there, I'll end up finalising the move-in arrangements.'

Garrett nodded solemnly.

'It's a job for a seriously sober man,' he said.

'Definitely. So, on swift reflection I reckon I'll leave it until some time tomorrow. Tonight I'll go home and turn in early.' Mike looked at his watch. 'I think I should ring the DCS and tell him what you've told me. He likes to be kept in the picture.'

Derek Bingham was still in his office. He took the news glumly.

'Hell's bells,' he sighed, 'I smell something messy.'

'So do I,' Mike said.

'What ever happened to good old-fashioned impulse killing? You knew where you were with that.'

'Absolutely.'

'And the murderers were easy to track down. They were usually walking around covered in blood, looking for somebody to confess to.'

'We've a team out now checking on Gopal's last known movements,' Mike said. 'I'll keep you informed.'

'Fine. Thanks for the call, Mike.'

'There's one other thing, sir.'

'What?'

'I haven't figured out why women yawn as soon as they wake up.'

'It's obvious,' Bingham said. 'They've no balls to scratch, have they?'

FOUR

The Buck and Ferret was a dark ill-ventilated pub near the centre of the city, a free-standing building once condemned and scheduled for demolition because of structural unsoundness and chronic rodent infestation. The enterprising owner, a recluse who hadn't set eyes on the pub for forty years, found a clause in the local property regulations that permitted him to keep the place open for business, so long as he did no more than *take measures* to hold up the structure and control the infestation.

Nowadays the Buck and Ferret had a permanent girdle of scaffolding. In the cellar and attic were a total of thirty rat traps. The pub prospered, being popular with shy immigrants and the kind of downhill drinkers whose appearance drew attention to them in brighter places. The main room was wide and windowless; it had brown-painted walls and a low sooty ceiling. Saturday was always the busiest day, so although they had been open for less than an hour the place was packed and the air was fogged with smoke. Mike squeezed himself in at the end of the bar while DC Chinnery spoke to the barman.

'Are you Rick Andrews?'

The barman grew taller by an inch. He was fat and oily-haired with bluebirds tattooed on his hands. His chin pressed back towards his neck.

'What's it to you?' A belligerent response was obligatory. It was that kind of place. 'I'm here to serve drinks, not answer questions.'

24

'I'm Detective Constable Chinnery. This is Detective Inspector Fletcher.'

'I see.' The man's expression switched to complicity with no apparent effort. 'What can I do for you?'

'I believe you spoke to a uniformed constable last night. About Mr Gopal, the Asian who was murdered.'

'That's right. The PC showed me the description and I sussed it right away. Gopal. That's what I knew him as. His first name was harder to remember, but I'd no trouble with Gopal so that's what I always called him. Came in here weekends, usually. Him and his mate. What's the story behind the murder, then? Any clues yet?'

'Nothing we can talk about,' Mike said. 'Tell me, were they always together, Gopal and his friend?'

'Always.'

'What did the other man look like?'

'Well.' Andrews rubbed his bristly chin. 'He was a taller guy. Fatter. An Asian too, of course. Nothing too special to look at, just an ordinary Asian bloke like a lot of the ones you see in here. He's called Ahmed. With him it's the first name that's easy to remember. Ahmed.'

'When did you last see the two men?'

'A week ago, like I told the PC. Last Friday night. They were earlier than usual. And they weren't as laid-back as they normally were. I remember saying that to Colin, the part-timer. They were edgy. Carrying a lot of money, too. They had a wad each, a big one.'

'How did you know?' Mike asked. 'Were they being flash about it?'

'No. I saw them handling it — you know, finger-counting it halfway under the table.' Andrews winked slowly at Mike, a prelude to a confidence. 'People don't realise how much you notice after a year or two in this job.'

'It was definitely Friday night?' Chinnery said. 'You didn't see them at all after that?'

'No. As a matter of fact I was surprised. Well not surprised,

25

but you know, I *noticed* they didn't come in on Saturday or Sunday. You get to know punters' movements, they've all got their routines.'

'Did they speak to anybody else while they were here on Friday?' Mike said. 'Apart from passing chat, I mean.'

'They talked with Ross Carpenter. I saw Gopal waving him over to their table in the corner there. Carpenter sat down for about ten minutes. He had a drink with them, then he got up and circulated for a bit. When Gopal and Ahmed left about an hour after that, Carpenter went with them.'

'So tell us who Carpenter is,' Mike said.

Andrews looked from one man to the other, savouring the moment. He leaned forward.

'Carpenter's a bouncer,' he said. 'At Revels. Know it?'

Both detectives nodded. Revels was a club frequented mainly by mature pleasure-seekers of a kind unlikely to find much pleasure anywhere, certainly not in each other's company. The membership teemed with widows, widowers, divorcees, restless husbands and disheartened wives. Mike Fletcher had gone there one night to observe the movements of a pickpocket. He had found the noisy, grimacing insecurity of the men and the herded loneliness of the women too sad to endure.

'Do you know this Carpenter personally?' Chinnery said.

'Only to nod to. I know *about* him, mind you.' The wink again as Andrews bent close. 'His sideline, for instance.'

'Which is?'

'Peddling.'

'A specialist, is he?'

'No. He'll deal just about anything you want. So I'm told.'

'Does he sell stuff in here?' Mike said.

'Aw, come on . . . ' Andrews looked affronted. 'I know we're a bit of a crap-hole, but the guv'nor doesn't stand for anything like that.'

'So Carpenter's never here on business?'

'I didn't say that.' Andrews tapped the side of his nose. 'It

26

could be he sets up deals in here, it'd be hard to stop him. But there's no actual trading on the premises.'

Now it was Mike who leaned close.

'In your own judgement, Mr Andrews, would you say the two Asians had agreed a deal with Carpenter that night, and when they left they were perhaps going outside to make the transaction?'

'It crossed my mind as a possibility, yeah.'

'Does Carpenter often leave here with people?'

'Always arrives on his own,' Andrews said, 'but hardly ever leaves that way.'

'So you've no doubt, no *real* doubt, that he uses this place as a contact point for some of his drug deals?'

'I wouldn't go on the record as saying so.' Andrews raised a finger and made a swift sideways slicing motion at his throat. 'In conversation, though, and purely as a privately held opinion, I've got to say I'm bloody positive this is one of his customer terminals.'

Mike stood away from the bar.

'I'm grateful for your help,' he said. 'I don't suppose you know where Carpenter lives?'

'Haven't a clue, Inspector.'

'Well, thanks anyway.'

'Any time. Any time at all.'

Out on the street Mike told Jim Chinnery to get hold of Ross Carpenter's address.

'They'll have it at Revels. Don't ask for it outright. In fact don't ask at all. Wait for your chance and snoop.'

'What do I say I'm there for?'

'Use your imagination. When that job's done, get on to Gopal's boss and try to find out who this Ahmed is.' Mike looked at his watch. 'I'll need to get my skates on. I've a quickie lunch date. See you back at the station.'

When he got to Barney's Baked Potato, Kate was already there.

'I ordered you the same as I'm having,' she said as he

27

squeezed into the plastic chair. 'Baked spud with mince and thick gravy filling.'

'Fine.'

She was scrutinising his face already, reading him. Or he thought she was. Maybe he just expected it.

'So.' She put her elbows on the table and laid one hand on the back of the other. Mike recognised the technique: symmetrical confrontation. 'What happened last night?' she said.

'We've got a murder investigation on.'

'I know. You told me on the 'phone. You didn't tell me it was going to tie you up the whole night.'

'One thing led to another and I got swamped. It happens, Kate.'

'I believe you've been avoiding me.'

'If that was the case I wouldn't have called and suggested lunch, would I?'

'To be precise,' Kate said, 'I believe you've been avoiding an intimate meeting where we could get down to discussing your — *our* plans.' She waved a hand, encompassing the racket and bustle around them. 'Here, you feel safer. Hubbub works against tension. It chokes off any chance of an uncomfortable scene.'

Mike squirmed in his chair. He stared at the dessert counter. Of all the women he could have turned to for companionship, it still sometimes startled him that he had involved himself with a know-it-all psychiatrist.

'So I'm right,' Kate said. 'You've had second thoughts.'

'My first thoughts weren't too sound. For a start, I was pissed on Thursday night.'

'You sounded sober enough to me.'

'That's because you were pissed, too.'

'Tell me what it is,' Kate snapped. 'Come out with it nice and straight.'

'Come out with what?'

'You know what. *Why* can't you make yourself move in with me? We've been close for two years, and for more than a year

28

we've talked about living together. Now it comes to doing it you're like a jumpy virgin on the first night. What's wrong, Mike? Is it me? Is it something about me you haven't been able to admit? Something that worries you or repels you, or what?'

'It's . . . ' He shrugged. 'It's like deciding to stop drinking.'

'Eh?'

'A brilliant idea, really. As an idea. But to do it, to put it into action — to make teetotalism a fact of your existence after alcohol's been a staple of your life for a substantial number of years . . . '

'You foresee living with me as a kind of abstinence, then,' Kate said coldly. She was sitting back in her chair now, staring at him. 'It's not something in the nature of a gain. It's a loss. Something taken away. A deduction.'

'I was trying to explain the difference between the idea and the reality, that's all. You don't have to make psychiatric evaluations out of every bloody thing I say, you know.'

'You've as good as told me you can't change. You're too habituated to the life you lead.'

'If you'll give me the chance,' Mike said, 'I'll say more than that. It's not as if I haven't considered everything. I've thought about it. Carefully. I realise that if I moved in with you right now I'd feel like an amputee — '

'Christ! Now living with me's like having something lopped off!'

'If you're going to twist everything I say — '

'You're the twisted one. And I'm qualified to tell you that.'

'Let's not say any more about it here,' Mike murmured, noticing other people were taking an interest.

'Nor anywhere, I suppose.'

The food came and they began to eat. Mike finished before Kate was halfway through hers. He sat back and watched her struggle. She worked intently with her cutlery, frowning at the plate, forking tiny portions into her mouth. As the minutes passed her face appeared to be clenching by stages into a kind

29

of fury. Suddenly she threw down the knife and fork, stood up and strode away from the table.

'Kate? Hang on . . .'

Mike turned and watched her push her way through the tables and flounce out on to the street. A woman behind him whispered something, making another woman giggle.

FIVE

Before Mani Chandra opened his mouth he always considered what he would say. That meant he spoke with confidence. To some people — mostly other Asians — it made him sound overweening and pedantic. He was thought to be aloof, too, because of his fastidious professorial manner and the immaculacy of his suits and handmade shirts. Sitting before DCS Bingham's desk, the dapper little man was the image of civilised concern. His hands were folded on his knees and he leaned forward, his head fractionally inclined as he listened to Bingham.

'A lot of these letters have been floating about lately. They've been sent to senior police officers, council officials and Asian community leaders like yourself. We've several on file. It's the same old song in all of them, Mr Chandra, and really I have to say they're nothing new. We'll always be plagued by people with misplaced anxieties and ill-focused resentments.' Bingham flipped the letter on to the desk. 'I really don't think you should worry.'

Mr Chandra slowly moistened his lips. He sat up in his chair, fixing Bingham with intelligent dark eyes.

'I think you will agree, sir, that a certain amount of worry is inevitable.'

'Oh yes, of course.'

'The letter was addressed to me personally, and although I have noted that the terms of its warnings are general, I still feel, unavoidably, that a measure of personal threat is implied.'

'Indeed. But a threat's one thing, carrying it out's quite another.'

'I would remind you an Asian man has already been killed.'

'I don't think there's a connection.'

'But can you be sure?'

Derek Bingham shrugged.

'No one can be sure. But I have to take a sensible line, I can't act on the basis of outside possibilities . . . ' He cleared his throat noisily, wishing Chandra would at least blink now and again. There was a sharp knock on the door, an answer to an unvoiced prayer. 'Come in,' Bingham called, making an apologetic face to Mr Chandra.

Mike Fletcher came in, flapping a sheet of computer paper. He saw the two of them at the desk and made to back out again. 'It's all right, Mike,' Bingham said quickly, 'this is only an informal chat.' He stood up and introduced the two men. 'Mr Chandra's chairman of the Asian Residents' Association.'

'And secretary of the Immigrants' Accommodation Service,' Chandra added, standing to shake hands with Mike. 'I am also in trade locally — I import foodstuffs from the Punjab and Kashmir. I believe we met some time ago, Inspector, when there was a break-in at my warehouse.'

Mike remembered.

'About three years ago, sir. We caught the men.'

'Indeed you did. I was most gratified.'

'Mr Chandra's here because he's had one of those crank letters,' Bingham said, trying to transmit a complex message with his eyes. 'I've told him we don't believe the threats should be taken seriously.'

Mike did his best to look noncommittal.

'We're not being complacent, of course,' he said.

'I am happy to hear that.' Chandra smiled. 'None of us can know much until we are rid of complacency.'

'That's absolutely true,' Mike said.

'The words are Mao Tse-tung's. I am no enthusiast of the man, but he did have the occasional illuminating insight.' Chandra smoothed his gold silk tie. 'I was explaining to the Chief Superintendent that although I am capable of being calm

32

and objective about anonymous threats, I cannot afford to assume I am safe, or that my friends are. When you arrived Inspector, I was on the point of explaining that I am forming a vigilante group . . . '

Chandra paused as both policemen frowned at him.

'I am not proposing a team armed with pick handles — or armed with anything, for that matter.'

'I'm relieved to hear it,' Bingham said.

'I simply plan to organise a number of alert and responsible members of the Asian community to patrol the districts where we live and where our businesses are located. It would be simple and discreet *vigilance*, no more than that. If we did see anything strange or out of the ordinary we would of course report it to the police.'

'We're never happy about vigilantes,' Bingham said. 'They can get out of hand. They make some terrible mistakes, too.'

'Not my group,' Chandra said firmly. 'They would behave exactly as I say, I promise you that. They would be in operation only until such time as Mr Gopal's murder is solved and the community can feel there is no cause for concern.'

'In that case you *must* impress on your people that they have to stay within the law . . . '

'Of course.'

'And they've got to alert us at the first hint of trouble. They aren't empowered to do anything on their own.'

'I will see to all that,' Mr Chandra promised. 'Please understand, Chief Superintendent, I aim to do no more than protect myself and my friends.' He pointed to the letter on the desk. 'I will leave that with you to add to your collection.' He smiled tightly. 'I imagine you have business to attend to. Thank you for your time.'

Bingham saw him to the outer office. He came back looking morose.

'That's the start of it,' he said, shutting the door. 'They're jumpy. They know about the letters, they know about Gopal being stiffed, so they've got grounds for a bit of ferment. First it's vigilantes, next it'll be ad hoc committees, formal complaints, petitions every time an Asian gets bumped at a checkout or pushed in a bus queue.' He went behind the desk and dropped into the chair. 'What's the latest?'

'We fed Gopal's fingerprints to the computer. It came up with nothing locally. Then we processed them through the national network and got a match in the Metropolitan files.' Mike consulted his sheet of computer paper. 'They had him under the name of Jimal Moraes.'

'He was using an alias?'

'More than one, probably.'

'What had he done?'

'He was an illegal immigrant.'

'Hell's teeth — you know what'll happen, don't you? The Asian militants will swear we made that up.'

'He was arrested in Southall for possession of cannabis. He skipped bail before his illegal status was discovered. He's been on a low-priority wanted list for three years.'

'It gets messier, doesn't it? Anything on his friend?'

'Still no trace. The name's Ahmed Faiz. We can't even get a fix on where he lives. Nobody seems to know.'

'But he *was* close to Gopal?'

'We've established that. They were longtime buddies and they worked together at the warehouse. No other known associates.'

'So unless or until we learn otherwise, he's a suspect.'

'And so is Ross Carpenter, the bouncer. Saturday he didn't show up for work and he hasn't been back to his flat all weekend.'

'Do you think he's done a runner?'

'It doesn't look like it. Neighbours and a couple of local shopkeepers say he quite often goes away at weekends, and nobody's seen anything being moved out of his place.'

'CID should join hands and pray he turns up soon, then. We need a collar, Mike. Carpenter sounds a better candidate than the missing Asian.'

'As soon as he appears I'll be on to it. I've got a watch on his place and they've orders to let me know when he shows.'

'Fine.'

'That's all there is for now.'

'Right. Keep me fed, as and when.' Bingham scratched his stomach and threw a disgruntled look at the window. 'What kind of weekend did you have?'

'I worked Saturday and half of yesterday. Went to bed early last night. Yourself?'

'Saturday night was the high spot, I suppose. Dinner at the Exeter Grill with the chief constable and other luminaries of the plod persuasion.'

'I envy you.'

'No you don't.'

'I was trying to say the right thing, sir. I know how you relish the ill-concealed resentment of subordinates.'

'Strictly *entre nous*, Michael, after half an hour I began to think my good nature wouldn't hold up. The *tedium*. I had to stay off the vino because of the driving, which didn't help.'

'What was the occasion?'

'Chief Officers' Association annual junket.'

'I've heard about those. Lots of speeches.'

'More than you'd believe. The CC's theme was a real sparkler — new parameters of street policing in an age of increasingly violent crime. He's an anaesthetic at the best of times, but his press officer . . .'

'Is it still Pilkington?'

'I'm afraid it is. I could have belted him. He ground on for twenty minutes about the need for high-definition image-development in the force. It was dire. The chap next to me nodded off.'

'Pilkington's a bore whatever he talks about,' Mike said. 'I spent a riveting year under him when he was a superintendent at Southern Division.'

'So he said. He stopped me on the way out and asked about you.' Bingham watched Mike's face. 'Are you surprised?'

'That he remembers me? Yes, I am.'

'He obviously keeps tabs.'

'Did he ask about anything special?'

'He wanted to know if you were over the loss of your daughter. I told him you are. I said it to dispose of the topic. The truth is I've no idea.'

'I'm fine, sir,' Mike said, reaching for the door handle. 'Time's done its job. It always does, doesn't it?'

Going back to the CID room he wondered if Bingham had believed him. He couldn't tell if the truth showed. On the whole he believed he managed an untroubled surface, because nowadays he was in control of himself. There were no more surprise swoops of heartache. He had faced down despair. He had come through.

But there were ways he missed Moira now as much as he ever had. He longed for the sight of her and the heart-touch of her smile. He sometimes wished — not wistfully but intensely, as if it were possible — that he could hear her voice. Most of the aching was like that, it was sentimental and Moira herself would have disapproved. In time those little pains would fade, he supposed. At his core, though, was one raw hurt he knew would never go away: it was the pain of knowing that his most enduring affection had no living focus.

'Inspector . . .'

He turned and saw DC Chinnery come out of the communications room.

'Carpenter's back at his flat. Lookout just saw him go in.'

'Start the engine,' Mike said. 'I'll be two minutes.'

He ran the ten yards to the CID room, made a skidding turn through the open door and snatched up the telephone from the nearest desk. He dialled and waited.

'Psychiatric Outpatients, please.'

If he didn't try again now he might lose another day. One more day of contact severed. He hadn't spoken to Kate since she walked out on him on Saturday. She didn't answer her 'phone at home and three calls to the hospital had failed to raise her. But he wanted to keep trying. He hoped she wanted him to do that.

'Hello? Is Dr Barbour there, at all? Well, yes, it is important. The name's Fletcher.'

The cold-shouldering simply wasn't appropriate. She was his conspirator in life. They could argue, they could bawl and shout and fight like mongrels, that at least was communicating. Silent distance between them was no good.

'Hello, yes?' He frowned. 'Did she say . . . ' He nodded a couple of times at the receiver. 'I see. Thanks anyway.'

He put down the receiver and stared at it.

'Shit,' he said.

SIX

The building was in a scruffy sector of the city's southeast, an area known as Under-the-Bridges. A square mile of cramped, tangled streets was crossed diagonally by three fifteen-feet-wide Victorian railway bridges that rumbled day and night with freight and passenger rolling-stock. The snarl of thorough-fares was not so random and formless as it looked. It was in fact an interlocking group of communities with sharply defined borders. Irish and West Indian groups had settled to the northwest and northeast; Asians, mostly Sikhs, occupied a rhomboid of territory to the south, bounded on either side by native whites at various levels of embattlement or disposses-sion.

'Carpenter's flat's the three windows on the second floor,' DC Chinnery said, pointing up through the windscreen. 'There's only one door.'

'How did you get the address?'

'The way you told me. I used my imagination. When I got to Revels I didn't try to hide the fact I'm a copper. I said I was there to make the yearly examination of the staff records and the members' signing-in book. That made them look at each other a bit funny. Four years they've been there and this was the first annual check. I suppose they reckoned they'd been lucky.'

'Who did you talk to?'

'A woman called Dorothy Beattie. She's the bar manager. I saw her and the assistant club manager, a rat-faced little nothing called Tony Webb.'

38

'No sign of Jerry Grice?'

'No, but his name got dropped a time or two. I gather he's the owner.'

'That's right. He's something else besides, but we haven't figured out what it is.'

One of Carpenter's curtains twitched.

'Do you think he's nervous about something?' Chinnery said.

'He's probably just trying to see out. There's about an inch of dirt on the windows.'

They got out of the car, crossed the road and went through the stairway entrance. On the first landing Chinnery stepped into the shadowed corner at the foot of the stairs. If Carpenter should decide to take off he would be well into his stride by the time he got to that point. A well-timed foot stuck in his path would do all the braking necessary.

Mike climbed to the second landing and stood for a minute catching his breath. When he was ready he stepped close to the door and knocked four times on the scabbed paintwork. He waited for a count of ten then knocked again, harder this time with less space between the knocks.

The door opened. The man standing there was the same height as Mike but wider and maybe twelve years younger. He was thick in the neck and tight-mouthed, with a nose that had been flattened more than once. His hair was a half-inch fuzz. His pale blue eyes were at odds with the rest of his head: they were sensitive and mobile, altogether more intelligent than the face they sat in.

'Trying to bash the door off its hinges, were you?'

'Ross Carpenter?'

'What do you want?'

Mike introduced himself and flashed his warrant card.

'I'd like a word. Can I come in?'

Carpenter shook his head, inflating his chest a couple of inches under the black T-shirt.

'I don't let strange men into my drum. My mum warned me.'

'Fair enough. We'll talk down at the station instead.'

39

Carpenter's lip curled a fraction.

'Fuck off,' he said.

Mike's stiffened finger hit him a second later, precisely and sharply on the margin of diaphragm between his heart and his liver. Reflex pain jerked Carpenter back like he had been shot. He hit the passage wall and doubled over, clutching his belly.

Mike stepped in and closed the door behind him. He bent till his face was level with Carpenter's.

'I can't stand cheeky kids,' he said.

Carpenter straightened up, wheezing. Mike showed himself into the living room. It was dark. The air was tinged with the smells of old Chinese food and aftershave. There was a garish, expensive-looking couch, two unmatched armchairs and a sideboard. The carpet was wall-to-wall but unfitted. Empty takeaway boxes were stacked on a card table in front of the couch.

Mike stood in the middle of the room and waited for Carpenter. When he came in he was rubbing his belly.

'That was triple-o, pal,' he said.

'Pardon?'

'Out of order.' Carpenter sat on the arm of the couch, panting softly. 'What's this all about?'

Mike was staring at a poster tacked over the fireplace. It depicted the camouflaged combat trousers and shiny boots of a soldier; the boots were ankle deep in fallen negro bodies. The slogan underneath said AFRO-TURF.

'Where have you been all weekend?'

'Away.'

Mike turned.

'Where's away?'

'A girlfriend's. I'm not giving her name or her address, so don't ask.'

'Married, is she?'

'Something like that.'

'Very gallant of you to protect her.' Mike put his hands in his pockets and leaned against the wall. 'You can tell me something else instead. What's your relationship with a man called Jishrah Gopal?'

'Sounds foreign,' Carpenter said.

'Are you saying you've never heard of him?'

'Let's think about that.' Carpenter screwed up his eyes, overdoing the concentration. His face cleared abruptly. He gave Mike a mocking smile. 'That's right,' he said. 'I've never heard of him.'

'You were seen with Gopal and another Asian a week ago last Friday. The three of you were drinking together.'

'Nah.' Carpenter's mouth held its smirk, but his eyes were more serious. 'I never drink with foreigners. Especially tinted ones.'

'That Friday you *did*. In the Buck and Ferret. You left with them too. I've got a witness.'

'You've got a liar.'

Mike sighed.

'Do you have plans to piss about like this all afternoon, or are we going to make progress?'

'Listen . . . ' Carpenter stood up. 'Just because you got a lucky shot in, it doesn't mean you've any edge. You don't impress me, cozzer, so don't come the third-degree shit.'

'Tell me the truth, then. Were you with Jishrah Gopal and his friend in the Buck and Ferret the Friday before last?'

'I told you I don't know no fucking Asians and that's all there is about it, OK?'

'It's a lousy answer,' Mike said.

'It's the only one I've got.'

'You'd have been half convincing if you'd said you spoke to the blokes just in passing, or if you told me they'd tried to score some dope . . . '

Carpenter strode to the living room door and pulled it open.

'Unless you've got a warrant or some other paper that lets you stay here,' he said, 'I want your arse off the premises. Right now.'

'As things stand,' Mike said, 'if I go, you'll have to come with me. If you refuse, I'll be obliged to send a vanful of big constables to fetch you.'

Carpenter appeared to consider that. Mike decided he was making up his mind whether to run or keep bluffing. Or turn violent.

'Why do you want to know all this stuff anyway? What's the story?'

'The story is, Gopal's dead.'

Carpenter's face changed.

'He was murdered,' Mike said. 'Somebody's got to get done for that. Crime and punishment, you know?'

'It's got nothing to do with me,' Carpenter squeaked. 'I never knew the bloke. How many times do I have to tell you?'

'You're in the frame until you can sing another song, one that'll convince me you're an innocent victim of circumstance. Which I have to say you don't even resemble.'

'I know fuck-all about this!'

'You'll have to do better than that, Ross.'

'This is victimisation! You're stuck for a lead so you're inventing a case against me!'

Mike drew a slow, invisible circle on the carpet with the toe of his shoe.

'You never met the dead man?' he said quietly. 'Never spoke to him or his friend?'

'Never. Anybody that says any different's a lying shit!'

Mike read the anger and decided it was mostly rechannelled fright.

'I think you'll have to come to the station with me.'

'Why?'

'Because it's not an invitation.'

They looked at each other. Carpenter had the corner of his lip between his teeth. His moment to erupt came and passed without anything happening.

'I'll want my brief there,' he said.

'Really? So you reckon you need one, do you?'

They went down the stairs in silence, Mike in front. At the

42

bottom of the first flight Chinnery fell into step behind Carpenter. At the car Carpenter was halfway into the back when he remembered something.

'The alarms,' he said, getting out on the pavement again. 'And the intruder lights.'

'What's the problem?'

'I didn't set them.'

'Don't worry,' Mike said. 'Get in.'

'Don't worry? Christ, The place'll get done over if I don't switch on the security. You don't know what it's like round here.'

'Get in, I said.' Mike put a hand on Carpenter's shoulder, easing him down. 'Nobody's going to burgle you. There'll be a constable on the door for the rest of the day.'

'What for?'

'To stop anybody disturbing the men working inside.'

'Bastard,' Carpenter hissed.

Mike nodded, closing the door on him.

SEVEN

Jim Chinnery knew hardly anything about his wife's opinions and very little about her prejudices. He had no curiosity in those areas. On the other hand he regularly wondered what his mother would have made of a particular person, place or event. He considered whether she would approve or disapprove, condone or condemn. His mother had been dead for six years but it made no difference, Jim still submitted people and events to his memory of her judgement. It was a habit.

Once long ago the old lady had said something like, *It's up to you what sort of girls you mix with outside, but it's up to me what kind you bring over that doorstep.*

Dorothy Beattie would never have been allowed past the gate. In her appearance and comportment she was eminently vulgar, an amalgam of visual and behavioural shock tactics that old Mrs Chinnery would have characterised as sluttish. Jim guessed Dorothy had junked the notion of modesty long ago — if she had ever actually given it a thought.

'Know what my motto in life is?' she asked him the first time they met. 'Get born and die, and fill the space in between with fun.'

Today, although she was working, she looked attired for fun. She wore a red bolero jacket with a low-cut lacy blouse, a short black skirt and red stockings. Black patent-leather stilettos put three inches on her height. Her glittery silver-blonde hair was cut in a boyish style that emphasised her prominent cheekbones. More emphasis was laid on with plum lipstick, claret eyeshadow and plenty of mascara. The late Mrs Chinnery would have *loathed* Dorothy Beattie. But she fascinated Jim. She had the distinction of being the first woman to cause him a spontaneous erection.

'You're as good as your word, then,' she said now, leaning her elbows on the bar so he could view the shadowed gully between her breasts. 'That's unusual in a copper. I didn't think we'd see you in here again.'

'I'm full of surprises,' Jim said, and wished he'd come up with something less feeble. Dorothy made him nervous. He wasn't calm enough to sparkle. 'I was in the district with five minutes to spare, so here I am.'

Dorothy had made him promise to come back to Revels for a drink next time he was in the district. He had meant to leave it three or four days — it was bad tactics to look too keen. But it had been hard keeping Dorothy off his mind, and he was due to be in the area this afternoon anyway. The bit about having five minutes to spare was a lie, however. He was already half an hour late.

'We're always quiet during the day,' Dorothy said, waving at the empty expanse of tables between the bar and the dance floor. 'Tonight it'll be different. Middle-aged groovers all over the shop. Do you dance yourself, Mr Chinnery?'

'Call me Jim.'

'Jim, then. Do you?'

'Dance? No, not a lot. Only when I have to.'

Dorothy laughed.

'Like a compulsion, you mean? Like having to take off all your clothes in a crowded place?'

Jim grinned, realising she was laughing at him, though not in a way that hurt.

'I meant at the events I can't avoid,' he said. 'Official functions, things like that.'

'So you don't dance.' Dorothy touched his arm and winked. 'I bet you love to social, though.'

He noticed she had extraordinarily even teeth. He wondered if they were capped. A lot of things about her raised the same general question: true or false? Her waist could hardly be artificial, but it was improbably narrow. And there was the balance and proportion of her hips. The breasts, too.

'I don't get to relax as much as I'd like.' Another dog-eared remark, he realised, one of the same clutch used by every married man who ever chatted-up a barmaid. Moving smartly on he took a quick gulp of beer, did a lip-smack and said, 'You keep a nice drop of bitter here.' He hoisted the glass and gazed at the light through it. 'I'm glad I came.'

'I can't take any credit for the state of the beer,' Dorothy said. 'It's keg. Once the barrel's connected I don't have to do a thing to it.' She leaned closer and he caught her perfume. 'I'm glad you came, too.'

He kept his face half hidden behind the glass a few seconds longer, wishing he could control blushing.

'Next time,' Dorothy said, 'come round at night, about shutting time. We can have a good natter when everybody's pushed off home.' She winked. 'This is a good place to relax when you've got it to yourself.'

Another true-or-false, he thought. Did she really fancy him, or was she just getting a cop on her side?

'You don't worry about beauty sleep, then?' he said, accepting that his patter was hopelessly stuck in the banal mode.

'Sleep's never made me beautiful. Just puffy-eyed. The longer I sleep, the older I look.'

That was another thing — he couldn't guess her age-group, let alone her age. She might be in her mid-thirties, but the mid-twenties would be just as believable. Part of the difficulty lay in a disparity between how she looked and the way she sounded. Jim wondered if she's had some kind of minor cosmetic surgery; her voice had much more apparent maturity than her face.

'I might pop in around two some morning,' he said. 'I'll make it soon. We've a heavy job on in the district, I expect I'll be working late a couple of nights.'

46

He looked at his watch. Four-twenty. He should have been at Ross Carpenter's flat long ago, searching and sifting with the rest of the team. He downed his drink and stepped away from the bar.

'Got to go, Dorothy.'

'So soon?'

'Work. I've no option.' He buttoned his jacket. 'It was nice seeing you again.'

'Nice to glimpse you too, Jim-boy.'

She came round the bar, a big bunch of keys jingling at her hip. He caught another wave of her perfume — 'tarty' his mother would have called it — and felt his stomach lurch as she slid her hand into his. She led him to the door, gently pressing his arm on the side-swell of her breast.

'Be back soon, as the song says.' She swung the door open. Her hand was still in his, small and warm and tense-fingered. 'Remember,' she said, 'it's my turn to buy drinks next time.'

'If you say so.'

Incredibly, she stood on her toes and kissed him right on the mouth. It was smart and businesslike, but moist too, with a flick of tongue.

'Go get 'em.'

'Yeah. Right.' He was blushing again, backing out through the door, feeling his hand come unstuck from hers. 'See you soon, Dorothy.'

He hurried away, hearing the door bang shut behind him.

So what are you playing at?

He kept his head down against the wind, trying not to think. It was unavoidable. He thought of his bachelor uncle, Willie Chinnery, a man he had been fond of. At the age of fifty-six Willie had had an affair with a married woman living four doors away. A scandal erupted when the woman's husband found out and tried to kill Willie. Jim's mother often cited the fiasco as a typical instance of male weakness at the service of a woman's guile.

Jim wondered if he was being led on, like his uncle. He thought he might be. Which was fine.

47

How would Mum have evaluated this development? She would have gone bat shit, he supposed. There was no class of transgression worse than the sexual kind; she had always made that clear without having to spell it out, and this involvement Jim was approaching — that he *hoped* he was approaching — was entirely sexual. There was no question of spiritual affinity or any similar non-physical guff. Dorothy Beattie exuded unequivocal sex, and Jim was drawn to her by physical want. On the surface at least, the equation was simple.

As for guilt, he didn't feel any. To suffer guilt he would have had to love his wife more. He scarcely loved her at all now. The marital adventure had degenerated into a series of mundane habits. New territory was exhausted; the same ground had been covered so often it was worn into a rut.

'Change is the law of life,' he muttered, climbing the stairs to Ross Carpenter's flat. John F. Kennedy had said that: Jim wished he could remember the rest of the quotation. Kennedy's stuff was worth dredging up when you wanted to make a broad point. 'Change is the law,' he whispered again, fancying he could still taste Dorothy Beattie's lipstick.

EIGHT

Mike Fletcher strode into the interview room and slapped a buff folder down in front of Ross Carpenter.

'Sorry to keep you waiting. There was a recount.'

Carpenter narrowed his eyes at the folder as if he could see through it. Mike sat down opposite. He composed his hands carefully on the table and eased back his shoulders. He inhaled sharply, then completed the studied preliminary by tilting his head.

'You're a pissy amateur, Ross. We found enough stuff in your place to put a pubful of your kind away. If you'd had the sense to tack down your carpet it might have taken us a bit longer.'

Carpenter sniffed, flicked his gaze to the ceiling. Mike opened the folder.

'Heroin, fifteen grams,' he said, reading from the top sheet. 'Cannabis sativa, leaf and resin, three-hundred and thirty-eight grams combined weight. Cocaine, eight grams. Amitriptyline, ten grams in twenty-five milligram tablets. Methaqualone, in the form of one-hundred-and-fifty milligram and three-hundred milligram tablets to a total weight of two hundred grams. Various other substances in smaller quantities, among them Mandrax, Penthrane, ketamine ampoules, procaine hydrochloride and barbitone sodium.'

'Sounds like you emptied your cupboards,' Carpenter said. 'You must want a conviction pretty bad.'

Mike looked up from the folder. His stare deflected Carpenter's.

'You're going to say we planted all this?'

'It's obvious you did,' Carpenter said to the table.

'Your dabs are all over the packets and tubes and bottles. Your handwriting's on a couple of the envelopes. Not that we need any of that. There's the evidence of six respectable officers to say this haul was found on the premises occupied by you at Hunterstone Road.'

'I want to talk to my brief.'

'You haven't been charged yet.'

'Well bloody well charge me or let me go.'

'I want to run over the rest of this with you first.' Mike sat back. 'It was an enlightening afternoon for the lads. They thought they were turning over a mundane, sordid dope pedlar's pad. A routine job, a day like many another. Then lo, they made a discovery.' Mike leaned forward sharply. 'There's a lot more to you than we realised, isn't there, Ross?'

'I don't know what you're on about.'

'Your political leanings, that's what I'm on about.'

Carpenter's eyes came up from the table, narrow again, defensive.

'It was a surprise, I must say.' Mike made a pinched smile. 'I thought you were just an average scumbag. Turns out you're a Nazi scumbag.'

'Why don't you just charge me and get the fuck out of my face?'

Mike turned to the second sheet in the folder.

'One carton, ninety centimetres by seventy by forty-seven, containing sixty-three pamphlets and eleven hardcover books. Pamphlet titles include *Britain for the British*, *White Rights* and *Spectre of the Jew*. Books include *Mein Kampf*, *The Order of the Death's Head*, *Hitler's Elite Guard at War* and *A Fascist Manifesto for the Nineties*.' Mike reached under the papers and drew out a ten-by-eight photograph. 'They found this, too.'

He put the print on the table facing Carpenter. It showed him in a well-lit studio pose, wearing the uniform of an SS *Hauptsturmführer*. Carpenter looked away, sighing heavily.

50

'I was wearing that for a fancy-dress party,' he said.

'Of course you were.'

'A mate took the shot as a keepsake, that's all there is to it.'

'Sure, sure.' Mike put the picture back under the papers. He closed the folder. 'There was this man,' he said, 'a philosopher Hitler rated very highly. Name of Friedrich Nietzsche — ever heard of him, at all?'

'What if I have?'

'Well, he said that after he came into contact with a certain type of man — in his case a religious man — he felt he had to wash his hands. That's how I've felt on the occasions I've got too near society's shitty elements. It's the way I feel now.' Mike stood up, shoving back his chair. 'You're going to be charged with possession,' he said. 'We'll have no trouble holding you on that. While you're being remanded in custody I'm going to use what we've got, plus anything else we come up with, to put together another charge against you. A charge of murder.'

'Aw, come on! *Murder?*'

'You must have been expecting it by now.'

'I never murdered anybody!'

'Yes you did. You killed Jishrah Gopal. I'll prove it.'

'For Jesus' sake — '

'Do you want to hear the scenario? The one I'll put to the court?'

'Stuff your fucking scenario!'

'I told you already how I feel about cheeky kids. Just you sit quiet and listen.'

Mike walked to the door, turned and leaned his shoulder on the jamb. He slid his hands into his jacket pockets.

'A week ago last Friday,' he said, 'you met two Asians, Jishrah Gopal and Ahmed Faiz, in the public bar at the Buck and Ferret. You were seen talking to the men and drinking with them. Later you left the pub in their company. Not long after that, maybe the same night or some time early next morning, Jishrah Gopal died. He was murdered, and after he was dead his body was mutilated. Now I think this is close to what happened

— you lured Gopal back to your place on some pretext or other. Maybe a drug deal, eh? Peddling's your real trade, after all. Once he was there you doped him — '

'This is bollocks!'

'You gave him a drink with a drug in it that knocked him out. When he was unconscious you robbed him of a substantial amount of money. Then you strangled him. You mutilated the body and dumped it at the wharf a few days later.'

'And what was Gopal's mate doing all this time? Have you asked him that?'

'We can't find him,' Mike said. 'He could have reasons for avoiding the police.'

Carpenter was beginning to look more scared than angry. He half rose from his chair, propping his arms on the table.

'Listen,' he said, sounding breathless. 'Just listen, and hear me out, will you? What you're saying I did, it's crazy. I mean where's the sense in any of it? What would I kill this bloke for? And *mutilate* him — why in Christ's name would I do that? Eh?'

'You killed him probably because you fancied killing an Asian — after all, you hate them, don't you? And you mutilated him because that was what you warned you'd do in the letters you sent out.'

'What letters?'

'The death-threat letters. The ones that just happen to borrow the style and language of a certain John G. Tasker.'

Carpenter's face twisted with confusion.

'*Who?*'

'You know who Tasker is. We know, too. He's the American fascist who wrote a couple of the books and more than half the pamphlets we found in your flat.'

'This is mad.' Carpenter sank down in the chair. He put his face in his hands for a moment. 'We did business,' he mumbled.

'What's that?'

'We did business.' He looked up at Mike. 'I'll admit that.

52

They approached me in the pub, we talked it over and we did business. Outside. Nothing big-time. Two twenty-quid deals.'

'Heroin?'

'Dope — Cannabis.'

'And you did the business outside. Where?'

'In the car park. We'd done it a time or two already. I knew both of them. To deal with, that is.'

'What happened when you'd completed the transaction?'

'They went away.'

'And how come you were dealing with Asians?'

'I'll take anybody's money.'

Mike stood looking at the floor for a minute.

'I wouldn't do stuff like you said,' Carpenter murmured. 'Anybody that knows me, they'll tell you . . .'

'You've a record of violence.' Mike went on staring at the floor. 'And you've a grudge against blacks. Eight months ago at Revels you beat up a Jamaican so bad he was in intensive care for three days.'

'Yeah, well, he was a troublemaker. He got stroppy and pulled a knife, it was him or me. This is planned murder and mutilation you're talking about. Definitely not my league. Anyway, it's West Indians I don't like — actual niggers. Asians I can take or leave, they don't bother me that much.'

Mike studied the floor for a while longer, then abruptly he pushed himself away from the door jamb.

'You haven't said anything that makes me change my mind.' He looked straight at Carpenter. 'I think you did it. You murdered Jishrah Gopal.'

'No I *didn't*! Christ — what proof have you got? Huh? There can't be any. I never put a finger on him.'

'You're the likeliest suspect. So we'll sift the dust, and we'll get the proof we need.'

'No you won't. You can't.' The tremor in Carpenter's voice was a mix of exasperation and fluttering fear. 'Look, I'm admitting everything that did happen. I was there with the guys on the night you said. I admit that. I sold them a couple of deals of shit, I admit that too. I watched Gopal put his deal in that fish thing — '

'What fish thing?'

'He had it on a long chain round his neck. Always wore it. A silver fish, real silver I think, a couple of inches long with Indian writing engraved on the side.'

No such item had been found on the body.

'He kept his drugs in it?'

'Dope, anyway. Always cut off a chunk and dropped it inside. The fish's head flipped back, it was a lid.'

'So what happened after Gopal put his cannabis away?'

'I watched the pair of them walk out of the car park. That's all that happened. On my mother's eyes . . . '

Mike stared, showing Carpenter cold disbelief.

'I think you should phone your lawyer,' he said.

Later, DCS Bingham stopped Mike as he came out of the canteen with a cup of tea and an eclair on the edge of the saucer.

'What's the SP, as they used to say?'

'I've charged Carpenter with possession. And I've told him I'm going to have him for Gopal's murder.'

'How soon, do you think?'

'Never, actually,' Mike said.

'Are you being cryptic?'

'No. I don't think he did it. I'm just making the bastard suffer.'

Bingham looked thoughtfully along the corridor, absently touching his neat haircut.

'I'd examine the evidence a little more coldly if I were you, Michael. To me, it suggests Carpenter is the precise and actual toe-rag we should nail.'

'I agree he's a shithouse, and he's got an atrocious record. But I don't think he has the dedication or the drive to kill anybody — not even somebody that's been doped.'

Mike's belief in Carpenter's innocence was less than total. He hadn't studied him long enough yet, but the interim feeling said he wasn't the man for the job.

'On the matter of drugs — the lads found umpteen kinds at Carpenter's flat, but there was no haloperidol.'

'He could have used it all on Gopal.' Bingham exhaled noisily. 'Dig deeper, Mike. Either unearth another suspect or pile up enough dirt to make a decent case against the man we've got. Do *something* and do it quick.'

'Can I take it we're under some new kind of pressure?'

'Yes, you can. I've been sent a copy of a letter the CC got from the Commission for Racial Equality. They're kicking up buggery. The longer this thing stays unsolved the more chance there is of us — well, *me* — getting my scrotum caught in a wringer.'

In the office Mike told Chinnery he wanted a hurry-up on the hair and fibre comparison report from Carpenter's flat.

'Go to the lab yourself,' he said. 'Hang about. Be a pest. If they try to shift you, point out I'm desperate for the report and you daren't leave without it. If that doesn't work, tell the head chemist I know where he lives and I know how he worships the melons in his greenhouse.'

Chinnery nodded, apparently missing the joke.

'After you've been to the lab, I want you to clarify Carpenter's standing with an outfit called the British Movement. We found a membership card with his name on it . . . '

Mike took the card from his pocket and pushed it across the desk. Chinnery looked at the slogan alongside Carpenter's picture: OUR BLOOD AND SOIL ARE THE SACRED FOUNDATION OF OUR RACE. He turned the card over and read the small print on the back.

'The headquarters are in Coventry,' he said. 'They don't seem to have any branches.'

'Carpenter says he spent the weekend with a girlfriend in Lewisham, but the return train ticket in his jacket pocket was between here and Coventry.'

'I'll check his movements.'

'Also, I want eyes kept open for a silver neck ornament that might have belonged to Jishrah Gopal. It's the shape of a fish with Indian lettering inscribed on the side. The head folds back so that naughty substances can be stashed inside.'

'I'll keep a lookout,' Chinnery said.

'Fine. Sniff round the shabbier antique shops and market jewellery stalls. You never know your luck. And Jim . . . '

'Sir?'

'Try to stay in the real world, eh?'

'Sorry?'

'Part of you — too much of you — is elsewhere.'

Chinnery went out, pretending he didn't understand.

NINE

'At times my defects of judgement dismay me,' Dr Garrett said. He stared for a moment at the blue-white fluorescent strip above the dissection table. Its glare made the room colder. 'There's a despicable snob in me. He gets overruled by my common sense, but it still pains me to know he's there.'

Across the table Albert Coker was carefully removing the stomach from the body of an elderly man lying between them. He frowned as he worked, giving no sign that he had heard Dr Garrett. He believed it was no part of his job to agree or disagree with remarks the pathologist might make about himself. Especially when the pathologist had been drinking.

'Take this poor soul,' Garrett went on. 'Take account of the emaciated condition of the body, the history of hardship, the police notes describing the circumstances of the death — it all stimulates our sympthy, does it not?'

Albert frowned harder.

'Yet what happened the instant I saw the body lying there? I saw the tattoo on the scrawny chest and decided the deceased had been a man of low degree. A profligate, a drunk, or a thief. Or all three. He's tattooed and to my narrow reactive intellect that indicates he's no good. The reflex has stuck with me down the years. No amount of reason will uproot it.'

'We had a priest in with a tattoo, once,' Albert said.

'I remember him. A man with the reputation of a saint. He had a large heart on his right forearm with a dagger through it.'

'And a streamer across the top that said Mother.'

'Indeed. I took one look at it and straight away made up my mind he had been a defiler of altar boys, at the very least.'

Carefully Dr Garrett eased out a shiny purple length of windpipe from the slender neck and held it up with two fingers of his left hand. With a knife he sliced through the tissues that held the larynx to the structures of the throat, then pulled gently on the windpipe. The tongue and larynx dropped with a soft plop into the upper cavity of the chest.

'It's simple conditioning,' he sighed. 'In the old days just about every dead criminal requiring my scrutiny had tattoos on him. The prejudice was easily rooted — tattooing equals villainy. That kind of *reactive* opinion doesn't get less with time. It doesn't shrink with the growth of understanding.' He shook his head as if despairing at himself. 'I come to the right conclusions fast enough, but too often it's by way of misapprehension.'

He lifted the dead man's tongue and squinted down into the attached windpipe, looking for obstructions.

'Take tinted hair on women,' he said. 'When I was a young pathologist, only trollops and tarts dyed their hair. Now it's common practice with women right across the moral spectrum. But my first reaction remains the same — if the dead woman's hair isn't its natural colour, then she's a deceased strumpet.'

With a long-bladed knife he made six swift, sweeping cuts deep in the abdomen, then put down the knife and stood back. Using both hands, Albert Coker drew out the freed cluster of tongue, windpipe, lungs and heart and set them on the table beside the pallid corpse.

'It's not good enough,' Garrett sighed. 'The older I get the readier I am to judge on sight, even though experience has taught me I mustn't.'

'That's human nature,' Albert muttered, committing himself at last. 'Can't be helped.'

At the door Mike Fletcher cleared his throat to announce his arrival. Garrett turned and nodded to him.

'If you can hang on,' he said, 'I'll finish the job in hand.'

Mike came across.

'Anything interesting?'

'A case of starvation, I believe. Another soul who slipped over the edge of what we once called the Welfare State.'

Mike looked at the dead man's face.

'I think I knew him. Not to talk to. Most days he used to sit on the broken wall at the corner of Witney Street and Arundel Road. Always had an old brown dog lying at his feet.'

'You've got the right man,' Dr Garrett said. 'His name was John Booth. It could be argued his dog was the death of him. John doesn't appear to have had a decent meal in months, but I'm told the beast is very well nourished.' He picked up a knife and approached the body again. 'An irony of adoration, eh? So concerned about the dog's well-being he didn't notice he was starving himself.'

Ten minutes later the autopsy was over. As Dr Garrett took off his apron and gown he dictated an *aide-mémoire* summary of the examination to his pocket recorder, hanging from its strap on a coat hook by the door.

'Case of John Rushton Booth. No evidence of foul play. Generally the body was emaciated, with the beginning of a scaphoid abdomen and wasting of muscle at the arms, legs and buttocks. Stomach contents were thready and consisted mainly of mucus. The bowels contained little more than gas. Given these findings and taking into account the deceased's history of long-term deprivation and self-neglect, it can reasonably be deduced that death was caused by malnutrition, with hypothermia as a secondary cause.'

When Garrett had changed into his street clothes Mike suggested they go across the road for a drink.

'I've had a couple already,' Garrett said as they went down the steps. 'This waiting until after six makes me drink more. I rush at it, like a kid with his sweet allowance.'

In the Grampian Mike ordered two whiskies. Garrett rested his arm on the shiny bar and sighed contentedly.

'I don't know why I don't spend more time in pubs,' he said. 'Maybe I will, when I retire.'

'Cheers,' Mike said, raising his glass.

'Good health.' Garrett sipped. 'Why are we here, by the way? Did we arrange to meet?'

'No. I dropped by on the off-chance you'd be free for a snort.'

'And why did you do that? A matey impulse, was it?'

'I needed a compassionate ear.'

'Fair enough.'

They gazed around the bar, letting the first drink take hold. The Grampian was an inoffensively restored Victorian pub with an abundance of well-polished brass, etched glass and elegant porcelain beer taps. The customers were predominantly male college students and a few older, academic-looking men — Mike called them the fag-ash and corduroy brigade — drawn by the pub's reputation for serving fine cask-conditioned ales, some of them from obscure privately owned breweries.

'So your decision to live on your own for a little longer hasn't been well received,' Garrett said, facing the bar again.

'How did you work that out?'

'Why else would you want a friendly ear — *this* friendly ear?'

'You're a marvel, Sherlock.'

'So tell me about it.'

'Passive hostility has set in,' Mike said. 'Kate's broken off communications. I can't even get her to talk on the phone.'

'You muffed your explanation, then. Bad show, Mike. Didn't she at least try to argue with you?'

'Not exactly. She went defensive, in an attacking kind of way.'

'You must have made a terrible balls of your case.'

'I didn't get as far as stating my case. She wouldn't let me go on. Kept obstructing me.'

'Oh dear.' Garrett leaned his weight on both elbows, the whisky glass an inch from his mouth. 'Listen. Since you've tacitly appointed me your advisor and confessor in this matter — you have, haven't you?'

'I suppose so.'

'I think you should remember that I need to know the whole story if I'm to do the job adequately.'

'What do you want to know?'

'Well, you haven't really told me why you can't move in with Kate.'

'You don't know?'

'I think maybe I do, but I'm not sure. What I'm wondering, frankly, is are *you* sure? Do you simply have vague misgivings, or are you responding to hard reasons?'

Mike drained his glass and put it down. He waited for the vapour trail to disperse from his throat.

'One day I'd like to marry Kate,' he said. 'Or so I believe. But right now the way I feel is . . . ' He spread his hands, then he clasped them. 'I feel I can't — that I *shouldn't* — curtail the process I'm going through.'

'What process?'

'It's hard to say. It's a feeling. I've never put it into words.'

'Then try, for God's sake. I hate vagueness.'

'Well . . . ' Mike closed his eyes for a second. 'It's a feeling, or a suspicion, that if I take up a new life with Kate I'll be detaching myself from the past before it's finished with me. That's a very lumpy attempt at an explanation, I know . . . '

Garrett stared at Mike.

'This is about your daughter, is it?'

'I believe so.'

'What's the difficulty? Do you imagine you'd be betraying her memory?'

'More like short-changing it.' Mike shrugged. 'It's a jumble. I'm still attached to Moira. She was everything I cared for. Especially after her mother walked out on us.'

'I know.'

'I still get visitations — you know, the unbidden memories. There's pain, but it doesn't feel like grief.'

'What does it feel like?'

Mike had to think again.

'It's like the tail-end of a serious responsibility,' he said. 'The

61

instinct is that as long as Moira's around for me, I should be around for her. On my own. I'm not defending that, I'm only reporting it.'

Garrett finished his drink. He nodded to the barman, twirling a finger over each glass.

'The way you feel,' he told Mike, 'the way you *are* towards the memory of Moira — it's not uncommon.'

'I didn't suppose it was. Does it take long to change?'

'Do you truly want it to change?'

'Not with any conviction.'

'Then change will be slow. But it will happen. You'll know it's happening. You'll find yourself accepting the distance between what is and what was.'

The barman put a fresh drink in front of Mike. He picked it up and sipped.

'Anyway,' he said, 'the way I am just now, if I tried living with Kate I'd make us both bloody miserable. I do want to make the commitment, but I have to wait until it feels right.'

'Why don't you tell Kate the way you've told me? Ignore her obstructions. In the end she's bound to understand.'

'I can't even get to talk to her.'

'Making contact is a detail. Step up the effort.'

'I've been making the kind of effort that interferes with my work.'

'You could still try harder,' Garrett insisted. 'Anything will happen if you want it to.'

'Right, fair enough,' Mike sighed. 'I'll persevere.'

'And keep me up to date.'

They decided on one more drink. Mike ordered doubles. Garrett swallowed half of his at one go and gasped. Mike turned and saw DC Chinnery come in. He stood by the door, looking around, scanning the tables. Mike raised his hand. Chinnery saw him and came across. He handed Mike an envelope.

'It's the hair and fibre comparison results,' he said.

'What's the summary?'

'They came up negative. Wherever else Gopal might have been, he was never in Carpenter's flat.'

'I expected as much.' Mike pocketed the envelope. 'DCS Bingham won't be best pleased. What'll you have, Jim?'

'Nothing for me, sir. I've got to rush. Promised the wife I'd take her out for a pizza. It's her birthday.'

'A quick one?'

'No, really, sir. I'm late as it is.'

'Next time, then. Give Susie a birthday kiss from me.'

'Very good, sir.'

Mike watched Chinnery leave. He turned to Dr Garrett.

'Another mystery,' he said.

'What is?'

'Young Chinnery. He's up to something.'

'How do you know?'

'I've a feeling in my water.'

Garrett sighed softly.

'I've always admired that about you, Michael.'

'What?'

'Your objective, rational approach to detective work.'

TEN

Dr Elinor Webb walked into the medical staff room and dropped her briefcase on the nearest chair. Kate Barbour was working on case notes at the table. She glanced at Dr Webb and nodded.

'That was not my most fulfilling evening clinic,' Elinor said. She kicked the door shut behind her and stood unbuttoning her white coat. 'Social Services shunted in a so-called acute anxiety. She's seventeen, anorexic, got ghastly rhinorrhoea and she sweats like a pig. *Not* an anxiety case.'

'Opiate withdrawal,' Kate said.

'Right. Diamorphine. She told the social worker she was having palpitations and panic attacks — hoping, obviously, to get herself put on barbiturates. It was twenty minutes before she'd level with me. When I'd given her the lecture and shipped her off to detox, I hit the bell and in waltzed this greasy little bundle of psychosexual ordure, simply dying to talk about his retarded ejaculation. After that I went on automatic.'

Elinor hung up her coat and crossed the room. Her tread made the boards creak. She was a big woman in her early forties, heavy though scarcely fat, with a sturdy figure and agreeably open, regular features. From the cupboard above the sink she took out coffee and sugar. She filled the kettle, looking over her shoulder at Kate, who was still writing.

'I have to tell you something, my dear.'

Kate looked up.

'If you'd relent and actually talk to Mike,' Elinor said, 'life around here would be a lot easier for some of us.'

64

'What do you mean?'

'Your mood impinges on other people's, that's what I mean.'

Elinor plugged in the kettle and came to the table. She sat down.

'This is the common room,' she said. 'Rank, spiritual circumstance and the whole damned outside world are to be left at the door. That's the rule. Democracy and a general ease are expected to prevail, and they usually do. But since you fell out with Mike you've been like a snake with cystitis.'

'Oh, come on . . .'

'It's true. People can't talk to you. They can't relax near you. They're scared they'll get a fang in the arse.' Elinor folded her arms across her wide bosom. 'You've got to lighten up. Either that or stop coming in here.'

'You're inflating the case,' Kate said.

'I've a point to make.'

'That's no excuse.'

'Of course it is. Overstatement avoids woolly argument. And it's a consultant's prerogative to exaggerate. Where's the point in shouldering all this responsibility if I can't go over the top now and again?'

Kate capped her pen and dropped it into her pocket.

'I'm sorry if I've been casting gloom or tension, or whatever,' she said. 'I don't do it deliberately.'

'Nobody says you do. But you refuse to take Mike's calls — *that's* deliberate.'

'I don't want to hear what he's got to say.'

Kate didn't resent explaining herself to the boss. Elinor was free with information where her own relationships were concerned. She was seldom secretive, never coy.

'How can you know what he's going to say?'

'I know, all right,' Kate said. 'Take my word for it.'

Elinor eased her fingers through her wiry hair. She sat back, staring at Kate.

'You know what he's going to tell you, but you don't want to hear it. That's bordering on the neurotic, isn't it?'

'It's self-defence. I'm too fragile right now. I'd crack up if I had to face what he wants to tell me.'

The kettle began to sing. Elinor got up. She put coffee in two cups and tore the corner off a fresh carton of milk.

'Are you sure you're not just punishing Mike for something?'

'That too,' Kate said.

When the coffee was made Elinor brought it to the table. She sat down again.

'Remember Mr Ollins? You sat in on a couple of my sessions with him. He's a dainty little agoraphobic, kind of odd looking, with a goatee and a monocle. Likeable enough, after a while.'

'I remember him,' Kate said. 'Hard to forget, really.'

'The first time I interviewed him he told me, apropos of nothing to do with his condition, how he had once spent weeks avoiding a relative who was trying to bring him the news that an aunt had died and left him a lot of money.'

'Ollins knew she was dead already?'

'Indirectly. Weeks before, he'd heard she was ill and not expected to get better. And he knew he was a major beneficiary of her will, she'd told him.'

'So he knew, but he didn't want to be told.' Kate tilted her head at Elinor. 'What are you telling me? That I'm turning into a jumpy phobic like Ollins?'

'You didn't let me finish. By the time he spoke to me he had worked it out for himself. As long as he didn't *officially* know his aunt was dead, he wasn't required to make any response. Do you see? His static, well-ordered, *safe* existence could stay as it was. Above all, he wanted the familiar structures to remain in place, without alterations.'

'And all because the life he knew was preferable to one he didn't,' Kate said. 'Is that what you're saying is up with me — that I'm frightened of change?'

'It's likely.'

'Christ.'

66

Kate tasted her coffee. When she put down the cup she sat glaring at the table.

'So I'm wrong, am I?' Elinor said.

'Probably not. I'm not sure. My head's sore with thinking about it. I actually told Mike that *he's* scared of change.' Kate sighed. 'If I'm honest, I suppose it boils down to me wanting more of him and knowing there's a strong chance I'll get less. Or none at all.'

'Change,' Elinor said. 'Fearful change.'

They sipped their coffee.

'What do I do?' Kate said.

'Are you really asking me?'

'Yes. Really.'

'Talk to him. Take the saga a stage further, while there's still a saga.'

'You're telling me to go ahead and open the doors to change.' Kate made a mouth. 'It's no small step. Things might never be the same after we've talked.'

'Change has to happen,' Elinor said. 'You might as well have a hand in shaping it.'

Kate thought for a minute.

'You're right, of course,' she said finally.

'And you'll talk to Mike next time he calls?'

Kate shrugged.

'As long as next time's not too soon.'

In the teeth of disorder in his daily life, Jim Chinnery hung on to a few stable uncertainties. One was that most people had ridiculously high opinions of themselves. Even the ghastliest characters thought they were something special. He often wondered what would happen if they were made to face the truth. He was prompted to wonder that again after a fleeting run-in with Tony Webb, the weasely assistant manager at Revels. On his way out of the club, shrugging on his coat, Webb had leered openly and winked as Dorothy Beattie led Chinnery into her little office behind the bar.

67

That had been fifteen minutes ago, but the after-image of Webb's nasty mug wouldn't go away. Chinnery supposed it was because he had drunk more than usual. Drink magnified annoyances. Earlier, at the pizza joint with Susie, he'd consumed most of the wine because her limit was two glasses and he hadn't wanted to waste any. Then he had a brandy while she dawdled over her cappucino. After he dropped her at home he went to the Police Club and sank two or three quick ones, then sat for a couple of hours in a town-centre club full of misfits and stopouts, sipping flat beer, waiting until it was late enough to go round to Revels.

'You're quiet tonight,' Dorothy Beattie said.

'Sorry.' He smiled at her across her little desk. 'I was trying not to interrupt the bookwork.'

'It doesn't take much concentration.' She put a deft pencil stroke under a subtotal and flipped the book shut. 'There. Finished. Are you ready for another drink yet?'

He looked at his glass. When he arrived he had ordered a beer and there was still half left.

'I'm all right for now.'

'And you call yourself a copper?'

Dorothy reached to the table behind her and brought round a vodka bottle. She poured a good measure into her glass.

'That Tony Webb,' Chinnery said, 'is he your boss?'

'His authority stops at the front of the bar. Jerry Grice pays him to keep the clients in order. I'm paid to run the bar. There's no overlap. Why do you want to know?'

Chinnery shrugged.

'I don't think I like him.'

'There's no reason you should. He's a creep. Nobody likes him.'

'Grice likes him enough to give him a job with authority.'

'Jerry doesn't employ people because he likes them. He *does* like some of us but that's coincidental. You get a job here on the strength of how much use you can be to him.'

'How useful is Webb?'

'He's perfect for the job,' Dorothy said. 'His main priority is to make sure the place keeps a reputation for orderliness. The licence depends on that. So he smothers trouble before it starts. A warning from him's usually enough. If it's not, he'll let the bouncer see the offender out. If there's still resistance, Tony'll take the party out the back and give him a bit of physical correction.'

'Hard with it, is he?' Chinnery sniffed dismissively. 'He doesn't look it.'

Dorothy took a long swallow from her glass. She breathed softly through her mouth for a moment.

'He's vicious,' she said. 'I know he hasn't got the build for it, but it's true all the same. He's probably got a knack. And since he always enjoys the chance to hurt somebody, the job suits him as much as he suits it.' She nodded at Chinnery's glass. 'Are you sure you won't have something stronger? Maybe it'd make you change the subject.'

'I'm sorry,' he apologised again. 'Am I sounding like a cop?'

'A bit.'

'I'll have a drop of vodka, then.'

'That's more like it. I'll get you a decent glass.'

Dorothy came round the desk. She moved past him, trailing scent. She wore a short skirt again. As she moved her stockings hissed softly. Glancing up from her legs in a kind of fluster, Jim discovered he could actually see the darkness of her nipples through the blue material of her top.

'Now it's after time, we're drinking from my stock,' she said. 'No formalities like precise measures. Or paying.'

She took a shot glass from the cabinet beside the door and put it in front of Chinnery. To his shock she sat down on his knees and reached across the desk for the vodka bottle. As she poured she wiggled her backside, making herself comfortable. She turned with the glass and handed it to Chinnery. As he took it she picked up her own drink.

'Absent friends,' she said, raising the glass.

'Anyone in particular?'

'Our bouncer, for one. Ross Carpenter. I hear you've got him banged up.'

'That's right.'

'Can you talk about it?'

'Not yet.'

'Fair enough.' Dorothy raised her glass again. 'Good health.'

'Cheers.'

Chinnery put the glass to his lips and nearly choked as her free hand landed in his lap. She leaned close and nibbled his ear. He had a flash of recall: his third or fourth date with Susie, they had gone to a cinema and in the dark back row he had kissed her and put a tentative hand on her small breast. The memory was stripped of feeling, a lifeless echo. This, here and now, was the real thing, the granting of a forlorn wish. He was having a three-dimensional carnal encounter with a woman who was *bound* to be capable of inventive lust. This was a First Time.

'I'll be honest with you,' Dorothy said, drawing back but keeping her face close. She shifted a little, warming his thighs with her buttocks. 'I can't stay long tonight, I've business to see to. But when you showed up I thought, well, it's worthwhile hanging back a couple of minutes.' She kissed his cheek. 'To break the ice properly,' she added, and let her fingers move a maddening fraction.

His responses collided with one another. It was a jangle of sensations, an extreme relish, or zest — it was something beyond previous experience.

'Give me plenty of warning next time,' Dorothy said, and touched her lips to the tip of his nose. 'I'll make sure I keep the diary clear.' She winked. 'I like you, you know. We've got chemistry.'

'I'm glad about that.'

His voice was strange to him, a slow playback with flutter. Dorothy moaned. She put her mouth over his and her fingers kneaded gently. Chinnery dared to hope this was an edited trailer of coming events. He shut his eyes and gave in to the sensations. *This* was a compensation of life, he decided, an oasis in a desert of dreariness and uncertainty.

'Touch me,' Dorothy breathed at his ear. She took his hand and guided him. 'There. Just there. Touch. Aah.'

It was true what Uncle Willie had said long ago. Life, in the main, was a bastard. But there were moments, no more than moments, when it was all a soul could want.

ELEVEN

A note on Mike's desk asked him to see DCS Bingham first thing. He found him in the car park with his head under the bonnet of his Rover. He straightened slowly, wincing, holding his back with both hands.

'When I'm at home,' he said, 'fiddling with the car's recreation. Taking out the plugs and cleaning them, adjusting tyre pressures, blasting WD40 everywhere — I love all that. It's good for the self image, makes me feel competent. But when something's up and I don't know what to do, it's a bitch.' He undid the strut and let down the bonnet. 'Come on, I'll buy you a coffee.'

He led the way across the car park.

'There's a rattle somewhere low in the engine, I can't narrow it down any finer than that. It only happens in third. After about ten seconds it tapers off to a squeak.'

'No use telling me,' Mike said. 'I'm not engine literate.'

'It's starting to get to me. I sit there all tense, waiting for it to happen.' Bingham shouldered open the canteen door and held it for Mike. 'I told the mechanic at the pool about it. He just shrugged.'

'That's all he'll do till you ask him how much to fix it on the side, cash in hand, no paperwork.'

'Cobblers to that.'

At the counter Bingham bought coffee and Mike got two chocolate biscuits. They took a table by the window.

'Something else is bugging me,' Bingham said, carefully unwrapping the foil from his biscuit. 'Nothing to do with cars.

Or work. It was in the paper this morning, an obit on some poet that died yesterday . . . '

'Gordon Telleman?'

'That's the bloke. It said that when he went through his mystical phase during the thirties, he practised belomancy. The word's stuck in my head. Belomancy. Any idea what it means?'

'It's a form of divination.'

'For water, you mean?'

'No. Divination as in foretelling.'

'Making prophecies?'

'Or discovering the unknown. Belomancy uses arrows.'

'Arrows.' Bingham released air through his teeth. 'How's it done?'

'You need six arrows and half a dozen labels,' Mike said. 'You write something different on each of the labels — it can be courses of action to solve a problem, or options on how to spend a Saturday night. Anything at all where you're anxious to make the right decision.'

'And you tie a label to each arrow, I suppose?'

'Right. Then you go out into the country, taking your bow and arrows with you. Without looking at the labels you fire the arrows one after the other in rapid succession. That's all there is to it.'

'So how do you make the divination?'

'Isn't that obvious?' Mike said, deadpan. 'You take the advice on the arrow that goes the furthest.'

'Christ,' Bingham groaned. 'How do you pick up this stuff?'

'An unfortunate flair, I suppose.'

'Did you have a creepy adolescence? Were your folks always shutting you away with old dictionaries?'

'I wasn't that lucky.'

'Where does it come from? You're a fund of information on queer subjects.'

'I hang round the haunted wing of Moira's *Britannica* a lot,' Mike said.

'And you've a hell of a memory. Belomancy, for God's sake. Who remembers words like that?'

'I'll level with you on this one. I read the Telleman obituary this morning when I was having my breakfast. I looked up belomancy before I left.'

Bingham grinned round a mouthful of biscuit.

'You told me what a croquemitaine was, though. Remember? You dug *that* one out of your memory. I love it, but I've never been able to use it in conversation.'

Mike looked at the clock above the door and decided he should be moving. He finished his biscuit and took a swift gulp of coffee.

'I had the impression you wanted to see me about something more serious than funny words,' he said.

Bingham wiped crumbs from the corners of his mouth. His face turned appropriately serious.

'There's been another anti-Asian letter,' he said. 'Same typewriter as before, same paper, same cranky style. He wants to know if we're taking steps to control these people yet, or does he have to slaughter another one.'

'Could be an opportunist shot.'

'Of course it could. But who'd be dim enough to bank on that?' Bingham examined the nail of his forefinger for traces of oil, then scratched his nose with it. 'The letter has brought about a dismal development which I'll get to shortly. Tell me, did you get any more background on Ross Carpenter?'

'He was definitely in Coventry over the weekend.'

'That's a certainty?'

'On Saturday a well-known footballer opened a new multiracial sport facility in the Stoke district of the city. There were hecklers in the crowd and a press photographer got a shot of Carpenter bawling the odds. Sunday night he was at a meeting of the British Movement — Coventry police have a snout in the membership. Carpenter's contribution to the event was a pep talk on the long-term advantages of harassing kids and elderly people.'

74

'A charmer, eh?'

'Goebbels would have loved him.'

'So.' Bingham leaned back, both hands round his coffee cup. 'Can we say we're in a position to move forward?'

'Not unless I've missed something.'

'What's the snag?'

'The obvious one. Our so-called suspect was in Coventry last weekend, and we've nothing on anybody else.'

'So what? The last time Jishrah Gopal was seen alive he was with Ross Carpenter. That was last Friday and the evidence suggests Gopal died around then. Carpenter could have killed him and hidden the body, then planted it at the wharf when he got back from Coventry.'

'Except,' Mike said, 'the pathologist's certain the body was dumped long before Carpenter left Coventry.'

'That could be a red herring.'

'You think so?'

'It's not impossible, is it? Carpenter could have sneaked back here during the night, either by car or on another railway ticket. He could have dumped the body, got back to Coventry and made himself conspicuous, so there'd be a time-fix. It's not exactly a new tactic.'

'In real life it's pretty rare. And another thing — Carpenter tried to cover up the fact he'd been to Coventry.'

'He *seemed* to, Mike.' Bingham was growing agitated. 'This beauty is near enough a professional racist, remember. He's a duff-'em-up merchant, and he's a dope pedlar. Mix them together and you've got a devious bastard capable of a lot more than the obvious.'

'Sure, I know that. But — '

'Look at the assembled facts, Mike. We've got a clutch of letters threatening death to local Asians. In our midst we have Ross Carpenter, a rabid black-hater who's already on our books for half killing a West Indian. There are glaring similarities between the contents of the threatening letters and Carpenter's bedtime reading. And to repeat the clincher — he was the last person to be seen in the company of Jishrah Gopal, who is now resident in the city mortuary with a row of baseball stitching down his front.'

'I know how bad it looks for Carpenter, sir. But it's not a whole case.'

'Have you traced watchamacallim, Gopal's friend?'

'Ahmed Faiz.' Mike shook his head. 'We believe now that he lived with Gopal. On the fly, that is. He was seen around the place a lot and some of the clothes we found are a few sizes larger than the others. Trouble is, they're all clean. No chance of comparing excreted substances on the cloth. Also, nobody's been able to come up with a probable alternative address for Faiz. There were a lot of unidentified smudgy prints at Gopal's bedsit, forensic think they belonged to another man. That's all we have. There's not even a snapshot of Faiz, so we've only a vague idea who we're looking for.'

Bingham nodded sombrely.

'Now let me tell you about that dismal development I mentioned,' he said, pushing his cup away. 'I've been having my voices again. The ones from on high. They're not shrill yet but they're heading that way. The message is, either we get a result within ten days, or we step aside and let a specialist outfit take over.'

'What kind of specialists?'

'The usual kind. Eight or ten racially clued-up clerks, answerable only to the Home Office, with experience of interference at places like Toxteth and Brixton. They'll move in. They'll ignore us and treat our offices like their own, because they have that kind of cachet. No time'll be wasted in bulldozing our territory and chewing up the lines between us and *all* the minorities. They'll abuse the facilities, antagonise the manpower and — you can bet on it — just before they piss off without having solved a thing, they'll put in a stinking memo about our operational inadequacy.'

'That's a hell of a prospect.'

'I'd rather have herpes.'

76

'Ten days isn't long,' Mike said.

'It's all there is. The brass don't want metropolitan intervention, but they want protracted publicity even less, since it invariably leaves shit marks on braid. Press features are in preparation. Our masters are getting miffed.'

'The case was bound to attract the tabloids. You can't blame reporters for getting nosy.'

'Hah!' Bingham made a contemptuous face. 'I'll blame reporters for anything, on principle.' He sighed at the window. 'They'll have scoured the crime databases by now. Comparisons will be drawn and ingenious guesses put together. The Chief Constable's press office is holding off three muckrakers right now, two of them from national dailies. *And* photographers are hovering about opposite the station. A firm charge of murder must be laid before all that activity matures into print.'

Mike got up.

'Is there anything specific you want me to do? Or can I use my initiative?'

'Now I've alerted you to the position, I think I've more faith in your initiative than in my own. If you screw things up, though, I'll sacrifice your arse in self-defence.'

'I knew you were a traditionalist deep down.' Mike pushed back his chair. 'I'll keep you informed.'

When he left the canteen he went straight to the CID room. Jim Chinnery was on his way out.

'I'm checking up on four possible witnesses from the car park at the Buck and Ferret.'

'How did you find them?' Mike said.

'I didn't. That barman's been having a think since we spoke to him. He phoned in the names ten minutes ago. They're regulars who park their cars at the pub most Fridays.'

'Only four of them?'

'These ones left at roughly the time Gopal, Faiz and Carpenter went out last week. It's not the brilliant lead the barman thinks it is, but it's something to follow up.'

'Don't spend too much time on it. Concentrate on finding out who Gopal's local associates were, if any. I know the men with helmets have been asking round, but I want you to poke further under the turf. It might help to go back to Revels. Chat to the woman at the bar, Dorothy thingy — '

'Beattie.'

'Find out what she knows about Carpenter's dealings with Asians — and anybody else. Get gossip. I think there might be a connection between Carpenter and Jerry Grice, something beyond the employer-employee relationship. Nose in that direction, too. Grice is up to *something*, and his style kind of meshes with Carpenter's.'

'I still haven't met Grice,' Chinnery said.

'Then you've a treat in store.'

They walked together to the back door.

'We need enough to nail Carpenter, or to clear him,' Mike said. 'I want bundles of facts and I don't give a toss who you offend getting them. While you're doing all that I'll have some of the lads make enquiries round the outlying pubs, in case our detainee's a bit of a wanderer.'

'Where will you be if I need to get in touch, sir?'

'Right here,' Mike said. 'I'm going over all the notes and every piece of evidence. We need a reliable summary, a picture to hang on the wall. When I've made one, I'll drive over to the remand centre and spend an hour disturbing the balance of Carpenter's mind.'

TWELVE

Moira Fletcher's pal, Iris, believed it was pointless to look for a reason behind life. The force, she said, simply went on spreading, and in its random way it created people, baboons, fig trees and amazing imaginations. Things grew and blossomed, things died, that was all there was to it. In computer terms, according to Iris, life was WYSIWYG: What You See Is What You Get.

Moira hadn't agreed with that. An unashamed romantic, she believed there was evidence of a vast, elaborate plan in the universe. She was also convinced there was such an entity as the human soul, that it had only one age, and was imperishable. Compatible in most other regards, the girls had argued fiercely about the nature and significance of life, without either of them changing her mind by even a fraction.

Moira didn't make it to the age of sixteen. Her father, two doctors and a team of nurses had finally been reduced to helpless spectators as septicaemia bludgeoned her to death twenty-five days before her birthday. In the time since then Mike had wondered which of them had been right, Iris or Moira. Had nothing of his beloved girl survived the death of her body? Had she simply ceased to be? Or did her spirit cavort somewhere blue and open and eternally bright?

The questions assailed him again in a vague, heartsore way as he dialled the hospital number. For whatever arcane reason, thoughts about Kate Barbour had triggered anxiety about his daughter's afterlife.

While he waited for the call to go through, he thought of his own adolescent vision of passing-on. At the instant of physical death, the spiritual being was carried through a white pavilion, sedately and in silence, to be laid in an even whiter place of peace. There was no loss of awareness. Eternity would be spent lying in the light and the quiet.

'Psychiatric Outpatients, please,' he said when the woman at the switchboard answered. She connected him with a series of clicks and a sharp buzz. Another woman came on the line. Mike said, 'I wonder if I could speak to Dr Barbour, at all? My name's Fletcher.'

As he steeled himself for the cool, marginally regretful announcement that Kate wasn't free, he heard the little intake of breath, her habitual preface to answering the phone.

'Mike?'

'Kate?'

'How are you?'

She had wrong-footed him. He had to clear his throat.

'I'm, uh, fine, fine. And you, how have you been?'

'Oh, busy. As usual. To what do I owe the pleasure?'

'Well, I wondered if maybe we could meet. Just for a chat, you know? Nothing heavy . . . '

'When?'

'Whenever suits you.'

'Well . . . '

The silence was like something fragile. Mike strained to hear but he couldn't even detect her breathing.

'I could manage tomorrow night,' she said finally. 'An hour or so, anyway.'

Mike swallowed softly. This was what they had come to. Two people who had been close, intimate, finding it necessary to manoeuvre like new acquaintances.

'Kate, listen — I'm sorry. I mucked things up badly. Try not to take it out on me. I'd like to explain, properly. I'd like time to do it, not just an hour or so.'

'I don't know if there's much that needs explaining,' Kate

said, and he heard the stiffness come back. 'I think I got the facts clearly enough.'

'No, you didn't. I managed to distort the picture. It was an accident, that's all.'

Mike shut himself off sharply. This was going the wrong way. She had come on the line prepared to participate in a thaw, but the air between them was freezing up again. Too much indirection, he decided. Get to the point, establish something.

'Look, let's say Singleton's Grill, tomorrow night, seven o'clock. How does that suit you? We can have a nice slow meal with a bottle of decent wine.'

Silence again, then a little sigh.

'Well . . .'

'What have you got to lose, eh?'

'All right. Seven o'clock. I'll meet you in the bar.'

'That's terrific. Really triff, Kate. See you tomorrow night, then.'

After he hung up he felt relieved. And hopeful. The hostile silence had lifted and there was a chance of reconciliation. For a while he felt good.

Then, as he finished off the summary of evidence on the Carpenter case, it began to dawn on him that he had put himself in a supplicant position with Kate. He had made his anxiety obvious. It was true he'd been decisive and brisk when he suggested a time and place to meet, but he had made it clear he would jump through a hoop to get her acceptance.

He told himself he was imagining that. But his recall was too good. He had come on like a pleader doing a bad cover-up. It had been there in the tension of his voice, in his timing. Kate was a shrink, she was trained to spot things and make smart evaluations. When she hesitated over his dinner proposal, what had he done? *Jumped through a hoop*. So then she said yes — and straight away he jumped through another one — *Terrific. Really triff, Kate . . .*

That, he thought coldly, was no way to revive the relationship. If he went back as a kowtowing hand-licker she would let him. And she would take steps to see he stayed that way.

'To hell with that,' he muttered, feeling like a fool as he rose and put on his jacket.

Ross Carpenter had been asleep by the television in the recreation hall when the guard came to tell him he was wanted in number six interview room. He came in puffy-eyed and dry-mouthed, trying to improvise surly menace.

'Christ,' he said, sauntering to the table with his thumbs hooked in his trouser pockets. 'You again. People must be starting to think you fancy me.'

'People would never believe I'd be that hard up,' Mike said. 'Take a seat. I want to talk.'

Carpenter eased down on to the chair. He sat with his hands on the table, a foot apart, balled into fists.

'The trouble with your body language is the lousy grammar,' Mike said. 'Save yourself the strain. I know what you're really like, remember?'

'What are you after this time?' Carpenter demanded, letting his hands uncurl a fraction.

'I've come to probe your hidden shallows.'

'What's that supposed to mean?'

'There's a set of circumstances, one at least, that makes you homicidal — '

'Bullshit!'

' — I want to find out more about that. I need a clearer picture of you, and to get that I'll have to dig around in the murky puddles of your psyche.'

'I told you already, I'm — '

'It'll be like sifting shit without the benefit of a long stick, but somebody's got to do it.'

Carpenter's thick neck tensed. Mike heard the click as tongue touched dry palate.

'Tell me, is it simply the sight of a coloured person that gets you going? Or is there more to it?'

82

'I don't have to talk to you or anybody else.'

'Do their reactions to *you* figure in the chemistry?'

'This is harassment!'

'You don't have exclusive rights to it,' Mike said.

'To what?'

'Harassment, dummy. It's one of your specialities, right? You gave a little talk about it in Coventry not so long ago. A mini-lecture illustrated with examples. Like how to put the wind up old Asian ladies by bumping into them in the street or the supermarket, knocking their shopping flying and giving them the hard eye as you pick it up again. Or scaring black kids shitless with one-to-one threats they can't prove.'

Mike took out a notebook and flipped it open on the table. He riffled past a couple of pages and found the one he wanted.

'"A truth we must hold foremost in our minds," he read aloud, '"is that nature puts its guiding mark on every living thing. Medicinal plants bear anatomical resemblances that tell us how best they can be used to alleviate pain, just as poisonous plants have clear warnings of their dangers. Mankind carries similar guiding marks. The wholesome superiority of Caucasian man has always been evident from his appearance, quite apart from his history of innovation and advancement. Who can look at the Negro, and then at the Aryan, and not understand nature's lucid message that he should cast out the one and cherish the other?"'

Mike looked up. Carpenter was glaring at him.

'You've got a lot of that kind of stuff tucked away in your little notebooks, haven't you?' Mike said. 'Very high-flown some of it, too — I recognised Gobineau, Houston Stewart Chamberlain, Madison Grant . . . '

'Into racial studies then, are you?'

'I'm up on fat-heads who think there's a causal link between skin colour and certain personality traits. What I can't get my brain behind is somebody like you — a dope-dealer, a cheap bully, an all-round shitbag who somehow manages to reconcile *those* natural markings with the delusion that he's a member of a master race.'

'Are you finished yet?'

Mike shook his head.

'I came here because I need to put myself close to you for a while. I'm trying to understand how you can be what you are and live with it.'

I came here to interrogate you some more, but I'm still sore at the performance I put up with Kate so I'm compensating somewhat at your expense.

'Bear with me. Pretend you've a choice, if that makes it easier.'

'I'm wired different to you,' Carpenter said. 'You'll never understand me. Don't waste your time trying.'

The intention, a few hours ago, had been to come here and question Carpenter back and forth about the Gopal drug deal — time, quantity, price, location details, the exact words they exchanged — getting him exasperated and off-balance so that he might drop something new, anything at all that he had chosen to withhold so far. But Mike wasn't tuned for that kind of interrogation now. His only impulse was to needle.

'Was it maybe an event in your childhood that poisoned your personality? Did something happen, something to make you feel so inadequate, so deeply fucked-up that all your life since then you've had to invent inferiors and persecute them — the way you were persecuted, maybe? Huh?'

Carpenter folded his arms and fixed his gaze on the junction of wall and ceiling behind Mike's head.

'Maybe it's sexual.'

A perceptible stiffening of the already stiff neck.

'You're drawn to dark-skinned ladies — yeah? But they've a higher moral code than people like you. Too many rebuffed you, so you've taken against them. In a big way.'

Mike stared, watching the anger in Carpenter go from simmer to critical heat. It was easy to gauge the torsion in his ego and imagine it in the outside world, untwisting like a rattlesnake. He was a creature of violence, all right. But a killer? Mike stared really hard.

'Or did I get it wrong?' he said. 'Is it dark-skinned *men* you fancy?'

'Fuck you!' Carpenter roared.

He jumped to his feet, kicking back the chair. Mike watched, gauging, sighting barriers. Carpenter's mouth churned. Tendons stood out like cables on his neck. But he sat down again, his face crimson.

'We'll talk again,' Mike said.

He got up and left the room. So far as the case was concerned there was nothing to report. But at least he was convinced now that Ross Carpenter had never killed anybody. And there had been the undoubted pleasure of jerking the big bastard's chain.

THIRTEEN

It was scarcely midnight, but the late clientele at Revels had gone. The redolence of sweat and cheap scent mingled with resident odours — dusty carpets, damp plaster, the urinous tang of stale beer. Following Dorothy Beattie to her office, Chinnery breathed against the cupped palm of his hand and quickly sniffed; in relative terms, he decided, he smelt fresh.

'I promised I'd warn you next time,' he said as she closed the door. 'But this came up unexpectedly. It's an official visit.'

'Oh, my.' Dorothy got two glasses and put them on the desk. 'Going to be stern with me, are you?'

'I don't think I could manage that.' Chinnery watched her pour two large vodkas. 'I've a couple of questions, that's all.'

'Ask them, then. Get them out of the way.'

She passed him his drink and pointed to the chair he had used last time. When he sat down she perched herself on the edge of the desk, facing him. He tried not to look at the hem of her black mini, taut across her thighs.

'It's about Ross Carpenter,' he said.

'I thought it might be.'

'Can you tell me about his friends, who any of them are? Or any Asian men he might have had dealings with?'

Dorothy looked at the wall for a moment, thinking.

'No,' she said. 'I don't know much about him. We've worked together for a while, but we've never been close, not what you could call friends. I'm kind of wary of him, I suppose.'

'Why's that?'

'Just an instinct. I know it wouldn't do me any good to get

close to him. We've a good relationship, as far as it goes. Cordial, you know? Cheerful. But there's something scary about him. I've always sensed it — seen it sometimes, too, the way he's looked at me when he thought I didn't notice.'

'How did he look at you?'

'Like he would like to hurt me.'

Chinnery frowned.

'Not to punish me for anything, but to please himself. It's a look you know when you've dealt with men across a club bar for a while.'

'They give themselves away in bars.'

'In clubs they're at their worst. They don't bother to hide things they hide everywhere else.' Dorothy shifted her feet. She seemed restless tonight. 'If you want to know more about Ross Carpenter you should speak to Cora. She's been out with him a time or two.'

'Cora?'

'Cora Oswyn. She works here. As a hostess.'

Chinnery took out his notebook and wrote down the name.

'She's not full-time at the job, but she'll be here on Saturday night. If you want to catch her before that, she lives in a flat up at Melville Court.'

Chinnery added the address. He flipped the notebook shut and put it away.

'You wouldn't happen to know if Carpenter does other work for Jerry Grice, apart from being a bouncer?'

'No idea. Maybe Cora could help you with that, too.'

Dorothy's tone, quite suddenly, was impatient. Chinnery watched her take a sharp swallow from her glass and lean back on the desk again, frowning at her feet, cupping her elbow.

'Fair enough,' he said brightly. 'That's all I wanted to ask you. The official part of the visit's over.'

He knew he had been less than artful, the way he had quizzed her. That was according to plan. He had come here prepared to do just as she had said — ask the questions and get them out of the way.

'I brought this to replenish your stock,' he said, taking a bottle from the pocket of his raincoat. 'I hope you like the brand — I haven't tried it before.'

Dorothy changed again. She beamed at him.

'Stolichnaya,' she said. 'I love it.' She leaned forward to take the bottle. In the same movement she kissed his forehead. 'You're a doll.'

He couldn't think of a response. He sat there, feeling the feebleness of his grin, aware his cheeks were reddening. Last time, the meeting had broken off at a point where she had him paralysed in a kind of lusting rapture. He had spent a sleepless night, feeling ill, sensing metabolic chaos. The word 'gutquake' had come to him from nowhere.

In cold daylight he knew the experience at the club had fixed the way he and Dorothy stood in relation to each other. She was the boss, she controlled the mood and set the tone. In effect she cancelled his free will. The idea of being manipulated would have appalled him before, but in the circumstances of this relationship he didn't mind having his autonomy suspended.

'Before you got here I was thinking of going to Mulligan's,' Dorothy said. 'I'd still like to go. Fancy a couple of hours there?'

Chinnery shrugged. He had come to the club with no precise expectation, although his hopes had been high.

'Sounds good to me,' he said, trying to look enthusiastic. The thought of spending the rest of the night in a jazz cellar didn't chime with the fantasies he had entertained for most of the day. 'I haven't been to Mulligan's in years. Does Benny French still play bass with the band?'

'God, it *is* years since you've been there.' Dorothy got her coat from behind the door and let him help her into it. 'Benny died. A guy called Pete Prentice is on bass now.'

'Is he any good?'

'He couldn't swing if you hung him. The rest of the band's not so hot now, either. But it's a good crowd there, you can relax and lose yourself in all that noise. And they serve up the best middle-of-the-night food anywhere.'

'Lead me to it,' Chinnery said, feeling sadness pinch at his chest.

Mulligan's was a minimally redesigned cellar. The plain brick walls and an arched ceiling caught the racket of music and voices and rolled it back down on the crowd. It was a smaller place than Chinnery remembered — darker and smellier, too, and shabby even for a jazz club. The bar was a flaky plywood affair. There were no stools.

'One thing about a place like this,' Dorothy said as they pushed their way to the bar; 'they never need to turn on the heating.'

More than eighty customers occupied a space scarcely adequate for fifty. The band, six middle-aged men with light blue shirts and red bow-ties, played a ragged Dixieland selection from a narrow dais at the far end of the cellar. The clientele, meanwhile, talked and drank with detached vigour and ignored the music. Between numbers there was no applause. The musicians showed no signs of expecting any.

At the bar Dorothy used her shoulder to lever a gap between a fat woman in a spangly track-suit and a youth trying to catch the barman's eye.

'Hop in quick.'

Chinnery slid into the gap and squared his shoulders, making more room. Dorothy eased herself round until she had one elbow on the bar. The front of her body was pressed against Chinnery's side.

'Cosy,' she said. 'If we had a drink, this would be perfect.'

She raised her hand and a barman came forward at once.

'What'll it be, Dorothy?' he said, nodding absently to Chinnery.

She ordered two large vodkas with tonic. When they came Chinnery paid, noticing the barman wink at Dorothy as he took the money.

'You're known here, then.'

'Oh, sure,' Dorothy said. 'I've been a member for ages. And one or two of the staff drop in regularly at Revels.'

The intimacy of the wink had rattled Chinnery. It signified more than friendliness. The acknowledgement of a bond, maybe? Memento of a secret time? There had been something *dark* in the covert action of the barman's eye . . .

Chinnery took a sharp breath and told himself to get a grip. He looked at Dorothy and forced a grin.

'Great atmosphere, isn't it?' she said.

'Terrific.'

He could see a man edging along the bar towards them. He was tall and white faced, a ghost in a bronze silk shirt. His gaze was fixed on the back of Dorothy's head. As he pushed past the drinkers his mouth worked jerkily, the lips staying shut.

'I think another acquaintance has spotted you,' Chinnery said.

Dorothy turned and looked. The man winked at her. It was the same kind of wink as before. Chinnery frowned at his drink.

'Clive Berrisford,' Dorothy said. 'He's the manager here. He can be heavy-going, but there's no harm in him.'

When Berrisford was within reaching distance he put out his hands and squeezed Dorothy's shoulders.

'Little Dotty Beattie!'

She was drawn away suddenly, enveloped in Berrisford's arms. Chinnery clenched his hands on the bar to keep from pulling her back. He watched Berrisford slobber on her cheek.

'So what brings my favourite honeybunch here, eh? I was beginning to think you'd fallen out with me.'

Chinnery would have found it easy to hate this man. There were adequate physical grounds alone. His teeth were brown-stained and uneven. His mouth was like an obscene purple wound. He had pale leery eyes and lank, dirty-looking hair. When his hands moved on Dorothy's sides they did so like marauders, the grubby-nailed fingers digging at her softness.

'You finished with that Astill, I hear,' he said. 'Good for you. You were wasting your talent with a no-user.'

Chinnery snatched up his glass and took a gulp. Berrisford was an abomination. There was no unity to the man, he was a clot of repugnant parts and gestures with no civilised cohesion. How

90

could Dorothy let herself be handled by someone like that? How could she stand so close to him? Who the hell was Astill?

Dorothy murmured something that Chinnery couldn't hear, then she turned, still smiling, and introduced the two men.

'It's a pleasure to meet you, squire,' Berrisford said.

Chinnery grunted and returned his attention to his drink. He felt the momentary awkwardness on his left.

'Maybe it's my aftershave,' Berrisford muttered.

Again Dorothy spoke in a low voice, moving closer to Berrisford. He murmured something back, then they kissed — Chinnery actually heard the wet sound of it, the slob's saliva mingling with hers.

'Right,' Dorothy snapped, her mouth inches from Chinnery's ear. 'What's the bloody game?'

He turned. Berrisford had gone.

'What are you talking about?'

'You know what.' She was glaring at him. 'I didn't invite you along so you could play silly buggers. What was the idea of snubbing him like that?'

'I didn't know I had.'

'Like fuck you didn't.'

Chinnery was shocked. He glanced along the bar. There was no reaction, even though she had practically shouted.

'Steady on,' he said.

'You deliberately showed me up.'

'I'm sorry, I didn't mean to.' He wasn't himself. He was somebody else, making a stranger's craven apology. 'I'm overtired. Tiredness makes me moody.' He watched, surprised, as her expression softened. 'I really am sorry, Dorothy.'

She put her hand over his on the bar and squeezed it.

'I suppose I'm on edge, too,' she said. The anger was completely gone. 'I've been jumpy all day. It's PMT. I get it bad. The doc gave me tablets but I never remember to take them.'

'My behaviour can't have helped.'

'Forget it.' She moved closer. 'Berrisford *is* a bit of a creep.'

91

Relief swamped Chinnery. He drained his glass and made to beckon the barman, but Dorothy caught his sleeve.

'I think we should go,' she said. 'I've plenty to drink at home. And it's a lot quieter than here. Suddenly I'm not in the mood for all this.'

Excitement overtook Chinnery as they pushed their way through the crowd towards the door. *He was going home with her!* The night was working out right, miles better than he could have hoped. At the door he startled Dorothy by drawing her close suddenly and kissing her.

'Well,' she murmured, 'that was highly spontaneous, Jimmy, I must say . . . '

She kissed him on the mouth, her lips open and slack. When the back of her hand brushed his fly he almost jumped. She drew away slowly and pushed the door outward.

Chinnery stepped into the darkness behind her, hearing the blood drum in his ears. He was suddenly cautious with his thoughts, fearful of killing luck by thinking ahead. He walked to the car with his arm round Dorothy, listening to her humming. He thought of Susie and imagined her worrying when he didn't come home. The thought faded as fast as it had come.

FOURTEEN

In a house in the north-east of the city Gordon Beames was watching late-night television with his Indian girlfriend, a school teacher called Kadija. The house was owned by Kadija's parents, liberal people who did not mind their daughter having an English boyfriend. They might have minded that before watching television Gordon and Kadija had been in bed together for two hours, but since the parents were on a three-week visit to New Delhi they weren't likely to find out.

During a commercial break Gordon nudged Kadija, curled beside him on the couch.

'Fancy a takeaway?'

She thought about it.

'Will anybody be open?'

'There's a couple of all-nighters on the boulevard.'

'Chinese?'

'If that's what you want,' Gordon said.

'You'll miss a whole chunk of the film.'

'All the more reason to nip down to the Happy Garden.'

Kadija thought again.

'I'll have sweet and sour prawn balls and chicken fried rice,' she said, without taking her eyes off the screen. 'Maybe a spring roll to start with, if you can stretch to that. And some prawn crackers.'

Gordon got up, a tall young man, athletic and broodily handsome. He took his jacket off the back of a chair and let himself out. This was the time when he usually went back to

93

his own place, picking up a takeaway en route. Tonight he would stay with Kadija, but he still needed the food.

The air was cold and still. A light mist hung along the street, turning the overhead lamps to pale fuzzy-luminous ovals. The damp pavements were softly zigzagged with reflected light. Gordon put his hands in his jacket pockets and walked smartly towards the corner, working out what he would order.

Ten yards from the corner he saw a figure in front of him, blocking the pavement. Gordon stepped into the road to go past and the figure did the same. Gordon stopped.

'Excuse me,' he said, and made to pass again.

The figure moved with him and came a step nearer. It was a man, apparently wearing a cloak with the collar turned up. He was as tall as Gordon, but the apparent firmness of intent made him seem even bigger.

'What's the problem?' Gordon said, getting the tone about right — manly, civilised, not prone to put up with nonsense.

'Gordon Beames,' the figure said, spacing out the syllables. 'That's who you are, am I right?'

'So what?'

'You are a wog-fucker, Mr Beames.'

Gordon peered through the brown-grey gloom, trying to catch features. Nothing showed, the head was only a shadow.

'A disgrace to your kind, Mr Beames.'

The voice was mechanical in effect, measuring the vowels, depriving them of accent. Gordon wondered if a quick punch would do any good.

'Leave the Asian bitch alone, Mr Beames. Stay away from this district altogether.'

Gordon bunched his right hand, slid it up the front of his jacket to chest height and tensed his shoulder. Immediately a pain shot across his wrist and flared along his arm. He realised he had been hit with something hard. He had heard it, the *thub* on the knobby bone at his wrist.

He jerked back, clutching his arm. The shadow before him changed shape. Part of it was raised high and too late Gordon understood it was an upraised arm terminating in a truncheon. It came down again at speed. Gordon put up his hand and the club broke two fingers as it arced down on to his head. He heard himself roar as he was clubbed again, this time on the mouth. He fell backwards. His spine jarred as he hit the road. Blood ran salty over his tongue and on to his chin as the assailant turned and ran, clomping away into the mist on heavy rubber soles.

Less than an hour later, as Gordon's injuries were being dressed in the emergency department at the general hospital, the receptionist admitted another case. He was an Asian, the businessman and community leader Mani Chandra. His face was streaked with blood issuing from more than a dozen wounds on his cheeks, forehead and temples. Mr Chandra was distressed and clearly frightened. He could only tell the police that he had been on patrol as part of his newly formed vigilante group in the south of the city, and that he had been assaulted — 'frantically, absolutely maniacally' — by someone he believed wore a cloak. The marks on Chandra's face resembled claw wounds, a doctor said.

Mike Fletcher got to the hospital before 2 a.m. All the Southern Division police officers had gone, except for Detective Sergeant Graham Knox. He was in the emergency unit staff room. He had coffee waiting and handed Mike a cup as soon as he walked in. Mike thanked him, swallowed some and was gratified to taste brandy. Knox unstacked a couple of chairs for them and handed Mike his notes on the two assaults.

'The Asian man's been sedated,' Knox said. 'They'll keep him in for tonight — the wounds look savage but they're pretty superficial. He's just badly shaken up.'

Mike was too bleared by sleep to read the tiny handwriting. He handed the book back to Knox.

'Who's the other man?'

'Gordon Beames, white, twenty-six, a lecturer in applied physics. His injuries are a lot worse than Chandra's. He's got stitches. He thinks he was clubbed.'

'What's his story?'

'He was nipping out for a takeaway,' Knox said. 'A man approached him, same description — if you can call it a description — as the one that went for Chandra. He taunted Beames about his Asian girlfriend, warned him off, then thumped the shit out of him.'

'I'll talk to Beames when I've finished the coffee.' Mike took another grateful sip. 'Are you on nights, or did this land on you before you got off duty?'

'I picked up the call on the car radio and thought I'd lend my weight, in case it was needed. I'd just got out of Mulligan's when it came through.'

'Mulligan's,' Mike said. 'I've cut the occasional dash in there in my time. Or I imagined I did. Don't think I've been near the place since Benny French died.'

'You're not missing anything. I was only there because we'd a whisper about chemically refreshed types turning up at the late sessions.'

'See any?'

'Nah. None that I knew. I did see somebody I recognised, though . . . ' Knox cleared his throat. 'Don't think I'm running to you with a tale now, will you?'

Mike looked at Knox's big bloodhound face and took a reading.

'You're running to me with a tale,' he said. 'Is that why you hung on here?'

'I suppose so. And I'm only telling you this because I don't like to see blue-eyed virgins get shafted.'

'So tell me.'

'DC Jim Chinnery. He was in Mulligan's with the bar manager from Revels.'

'Dorothy Beattie,' Mike nodded. 'It's OK, I told him to speak to her.'

'With respect, sir, I don't think it's OK. They were more than a bit smoochy — at the bar and on the way out.'

Mike considered his recent feelings about Chinnery. The lad was distracted; it was just as obvious that his sincerity lacked a layer or two and now amounted to borderline deceit. Mike hadn't suspected it was anything to do with a woman. Chinnery didn't invite that kind of suspicion.

'You think Beattie's bad news for him, do you?'

'She's never been glad tidings for anybody I know of,' Knox said. 'She's on the game, apart from anything else. The bar-manager job's pocket money and a plausible front.'

'I don't think Chinnery knows that.'

'I'm sure he doesn't.'

'Has she got a pimp?'

'Grice.'

'Could you prove that?'

Knox shook his head.

'But I know it's true.'

'Dear-oh-bloody-dear.' Mike drew his hand slowly across his eyes. 'I suppose I'll have to rescue young Jim while he's still eligible to carry a warrant card.' He took a careful swallow of coffee, keeping the cup as level as possible to save most of the remaining brandy for the last swig. 'Tell me more about Dorothy Beattie.'

'She's got previous for soliciting, and there's a couple of blackmail charges that didn't survive as far as court. It occurred to me, seeing the way she was encouraging Chinnery and letting him come on to her, that she might be — '

'Yes, yes,' Mike groaned, 'he could be on a fellatio photocall even as we speak.'

'She's good at her job,' Knox said, without a trace of admiration. 'Known as the hostess with the moistest. Rumour has it that if she had to, she could suck-start a Honda.'

They grinned wanly at each other.

'I'm glad you've told me about this,' Mike said.

'I hope it's not too late.'

They raised their paper cups and glumly took the final gulp.

Mike's pager sounded. He went to the telephone hanging by the door.

'Outside line, please.' He waited a second then dialled the

97

station number. The desk answered. 'Sergeant Brewster? DI Fletcher here. You rang?'

He listened to the sergeant's hurried message, nodding, blinking the weariness from his eyes.

'Right. I'm on to it. Tell DCS Bingham I'll rendezvous with him at the scene.' Mike slammed the phone back on its hook. 'It never pours but it floods,' he said, grabbing his coat.

Knox was on his feet, re-stacking the chairs.

'What's up?'

'They've found another body. In the underground car park opposite the railway station. Male Asian. Strangled and mutilated, just like before.'

FIFTEEN

'As in this case, slashed wrists are usually on the left side,' Dr Garrett said. 'That's because the majority of people are right-handed. It's a kind of injury that's hardly ever fatal. The would-be suicide tends to over-extend the wrist, so the radial artery nestles alongside the head of the radius bone, safely out of the way of the knife.'

DCS Bingham absorbed the information with the trace of a nod. He had eaten nothing since getting out of bed in the middle of the night. It was now nearly midday. Consequently he didn't feel talkative. He was staring at the body on the dissection table, a young Asian male, seventy inches long according to Albert Coker's measurement. He had a thick mop of shiny, healthy-looking black hair. His face, before it was mutilated, had probably been handsome. There was a deep ligature mark round his neck and both his eyes had been put out. The right leg was fractured in three places, the left one snapped at the knee. The wrist wound Garrett referred to was an old pale scar.

'Maybe he was suicidal as a teenager,' Garrett murmured, pushing the head on one side to examine the neck. 'I know I was, from time to time. I didn't have the guts to do anything about it, mind you.'

Bingham surveyed the body glumly as the door swung open and Mike Fletcher came in. He had a six-by-four colour print with him, a head-and-shoulders shot of the dead man with closed eyelids painted in by a police artist.

'I think we've got an identification.' Mike came to the table and pushed back a strand of hair from the corpse's forehead.

99

'Yup. See, there?' He pointed to a penny-sized red weal at the centre of the hairline. 'Birthmark. Apparently he always combed his hair down to cover it.'

'So who is he?' Bingham said.

'Ahmed Faiz. Gopal's missing friend.'

Bingham stared.

'For sure?'

'Definitely. He was identified by eight people where he worked. The birthmark's just a clincher.'

'Marvellous.' Bingham looked down at the body. 'There goes our only other suspect.'

'Ditto the one we've got inside,' Mike said. 'Doctor Garrett reckons this man died some time last night.'

'Unless Carpenter did kill Gopal, and this is a copycat job.'

'Not a chance of it,' Dr Garrett said.

'You're that certain, are you?' Bingham said coldly.

'I'll find plenty of evidence to prove that this man and the first one were killed and mutilated by the same person.' Garrett waved a knife over the body like a pointer. 'I can *see* the MO is identical. This victim's eyes were put out with an object, probably a knife, of identical shape and length to the one that destroyed Gopal's left eye. The knots in both ligatures were tied exactly the same. The striking edge of whatever broke the legs was the same shape and was wielded from the same angle in both cases. I know that much from just looking. Wait until I've opened him up.'

As if that were a cue Albert Coker began laying dissection instruments in a row beside the body. Motioning for Mike to follow, Bingham went to the furthest corner of the room where an old straight-backed chair stood by a small school-type wooden desk. He sat down heavily on the chair, making it creak. Mike leaned on the wall.

'How do I look?' Bingham said.

'Washed out.'

'I'll swear I'm borderline hypoglycaemic. If I don't have something sweet to eat every couple of hours I start cracking up.'

'Do you want something now?'

'In a minute. We'll nip out for a break. Before we do I want a summary I can chew over with my coffee.'

'Well . . . '

Mike closed his eyes. He massaged the lids with two fingers. He hadn't been to bed and had only managed to snatch a couple of hours in a chair at the office.

'Forensics and twenty-five uniformed men are still combing the car park where Faiz was found. All staff and regular users are being interviewed. The lads aren't hopeful of coming up with much but they have to try. I've got Faiz's fingerprints going through the computer networks right now — we might come up with known associates.'

'And Spilsbury over there might find an image of the killer printed on the dead man's retinas.' Bingham yawned, rubbing his stomach. 'We're in the shit, aren't we? Two murders and nobody to hang them on. Two *racist* murders, God help us . . .'

'You heard about the assaults last night, did you? Mr Chandra was one of the victims.'

'Don't talk to me about it. I just don't want to think of the implications. Not yet.' Bingham looked at Mike almost pleadingly. 'Do we have anything going for us? Is there a glimmer in any quarter, however faint?'

'Right now, no.'

'In which case,' Bingham said, 'strange men will be walking our corridors. They'll be commandeering our desks and putting rockets up us before we know it.'

'Should we have that coffee break now?'

Bingham stood up. They walked to the door, nodding to Dr Garrett as they went. At the door Mike suddenly remembered his plans for the evening.

'I'll use the office phone on the way out, if I may,' he called to Dr Garrett.

'Be our guest.'

DCS Bingham went ahead to the café. Before Mike called the hospital he rang the station. They told him he had just missed

DC Chinnery. That was the third time since nine o'clock. He rang the hospital and got through to Kate straight away.

'I'm just off to lunch,' she said brightly. 'If this is a reminder about tonight there's no need — I hadn't forgotten.'

'It's an apology, actually,' Mike said, alert for any trace of chicken in his tone. 'Maybe you heard, we've got another murder on our hands.'

'So?'

'Well you know what it means, I'll be working till all hours — '

'They found this body last night, didn't they?'

The chiding note was unmistakable.

'That's right.'

'So you've known all day, presumably, that you'd be working late tonight. But you wait until now to tell me we can't have dinner this evening.'

'Kate, listen — '

'I suppose there was absolutely *no* time earlier. All those bloody priorities.'

'You've gone unfair on me again,' Mike said.

'*I've* gone unfair?' The tone now was indignant, going counter-accusative. 'How can you make yourself believe that? Just how in hell can — '

'OK, fine,' Mike said. 'For the record, what you said is right, I should have called you earlier. I apologise for that, *and* for having to cancel our date. I'm also sorry I'm too busy to hang around and feed your spite. Goodbye, Kate.'

He slammed down the receiver and stared at the frosted window. For a minute he thought of nothing. He listened to the pulse in his ears. Then without willing it he pictured Kate. To avoid wondering where things would go now, he turned and strode to the door. He opened it and nearly bumped into Albert Coker.

'Doctor wants to see you,' Albert grunted, and led the way back to the dissection room.

Dr Garrett was leaning over the body of Ahmed Faiz. As he

turned Mike saw the abdomen was open all the way from the throat to the lower belly.

'I've found something extraordinary,' Garrett said, beckoning Mike closer.

Ten minutes later, as DCS Bingham swallowed the last bite of his second chocolate biscuit, he looked up and saw Mike come into the café. He looked agitated.

'Your coffee'll be cold by now,' Bingham said.

Mike didn't sit down. Instead he put his hands on the table and propped himself on his arms.

'There's been a development, sir. Dr Garrett opened up the body a few minutes ago. Everything looked kosher, then he found ice crystals in the bowel. He poked around some more and discovered the spleen and the inner surface of the liver were half frozen.'

Bingham blinked at Mike.

'What are you telling me?'

'The body's been frozen. Technically, it's still thawing out.'

'How long was it frozen?'

'It's not possible to say. Presumably somebody thought they'd softened him up again before they dumped him, but they underestimated how long it takes the inside of meat to thaw. The really important thing is, Garrett's convinced the stomach contents are the same as Gopal's. We were pretty sure they lived together, and it's likely they ate together . . . '

'So maybe they died at the same time?'

'That's how it looks. Then Faiz was frozen for a while so his body could be planted to look like a later death.'

Bingham considered the new information in silence. Mike went to the counter and got fresh coffee for them both. When he came back to the table Bingham was frowning.

'Does this development put Carpenter back in the frame, do you think?'

'With a conspirator on the outside, you mean?' Mike shrugged. 'I've no faith in the idea that Carpenter's connected to any killing.'

103

'That's a subjective reaction. You could be wrong.'

'I know I could.'

'So confront him with this. Tell him we know the body was frozen. The grand scheme to slaughter immigrants and get away with it has backfired. Tell him he's shut his balls in the drawer.'

'I don't think I could be all that convincing. Not with something this operatic. He'd know I didn't believe in my material.'

'In that case,' Bingham said, 'we'll both have a go at him. It should do something for your credibility if we tackle him simultaneously.'

'Nice cop and nasty cop, you mean?'

'No. Two nasty cops. Pile on the pressure and the psychology looks after itself.'

'I don't like it, sir.'

'You don't have to,' Bingham said.

SIXTEEN

'Obfuscation,' Mani Chandra said. He put his hand down flat on the front edge of Mike's desk, not quite a slap. 'That is all I have been offered. I appeal to you for the truth, sir. I am candidly frightened. So are the people I represent. What is the *true* position in this case?'

'Can I get you a coffee, Mr Chandra?'

Mike felt sorry for him. His cheeks, forehead and chin were tracked with scratches. His eyes were sunken and dark rimmed. The tidiness of his clothing somehow emphasised the damage and the vulnerability.

'I would sooner have an answer,' he said.

'Very well. We have a man in custody. On existing evidence I couldn't say if he's the murderer or not. My personal instinct says he isn't. As for the person who attacked you, we certainly don't have him. But we're nowhere near being complacent about what's happened. A lot is being done.'

It was true. As well as checks being made in homicide data banks across Europe, the *modus operandi* of the killer was being measured against the behaviour of the man or men who attacked Mani Chandra and Gordon Beames. Parallels invisible to human investigators could be detected by the computer section's newest Intelligent System, a sophisticated program that learned something more about the quirks and habits of criminals from every case it scrutinised. If connections existed, even if they were no more than likely, they would be followed up by computer-matching of known felons to the characteristics uncovered by the tests. To the same end, less recondite

105

channels of investigation were being pursued by two hundred and sixty uniformed and plainclothes officers operating in all sectors of the city.

'Are you hopeful?' Mani Chandra said.

'We're always hopeful.'

Mike could have bitten his tongue the instant he said it. He saw the flash of contempt in Chandra's eyes.

'I'm sorry,' Mike said. 'That was glib.'

'Indeed it was.'

'The truth is, at present there's nothing to hang our hopes on. But hope *is* a habit in this job. We're trying our hardest to get a decent lead.'

Chandra took that in with a slow blink.

'So the position,' he said, 'is that everything feasible is being done, but even so, myself and my fellow Asians are still as much at risk as we ever were.'

'You'd be wise to take precautions, for the time being.'

Chandra sighed and gingerly touched one of the scratches on his cheek.

'It is hard to explain the — extremity of fear the attack has produced in me. I have lived with a certain amount of prejudice for most of my life, and I have never been indifferent to any of it, even the mildest manifestations. I have always been uneasy and occasionally afraid. But I have never known terror like this.'

The little man seemed suddenly too agitated to sit. He got up and walked a tight circle to the back of the chair.

'It *is* terror, Mr Fletcher. I am not the only one. It took a considerable effort to prevent a number of others from petitioning the police today. I managed to convince them that they would do no more than impede the progress of the investigation. But they won't listen to my counsel for ever. They are very frightened people.'

When Chandra had gone Mike decided there was time for a snatched lunch in the canteen. On the way he saw Chinnery ahead of him, walking in the same direction. Mike whistled. Chinnery stopped and waited for him to catch up.

'I've been trying to find you all morning,' Mike said.

'I got dragooned into doing SOC interviews. About twenty minutes ago I noticed the batteries in my pager had gone flat, so I came back.'

Chinnery had made an effort to look smart. He wore a fresh blue shirt, his tie was neatly knotted, his hair was combed and he had shaved with more care than usual. Close-up, there was a hint of Kouros. In spite of all that, Chinnery looked terrible. Mike told him so.

'I think I've got a touch of 'flu,' Chinnery said, looking away.

'That's what you reckon, is it?'

'Well, there's a lot of it about.'

'Speaking as a man with an eye for these things, I'd say you look like a bloke suffering from too much bed and not enough sleep.'

Chinnery overdid the eye-rolling. Blushing, he fumbled out his notebook and flipped through the pages.

'I don't know if it's still relevant,' he said, 'but you asked me to find out more about Carpenter's contacts.' He frowned at his handwriting. 'I'm told the person to speak to is a woman called Cora Oswyn. She's a part-time hostess at Revels and she's been out with Carpenter. Dorothy Beattie says if anybody knows about him, it'll be Oswyn.'

'You haven't spoken to her, then?'

'She'll be back at work on Saturday.'

'Got a home address?'

Chinnery squinted at the book again.

'No number, but she has a flat at Melville Court.'

'Get up there some time in the next couple of days.'

'You're still interested?'

'Why shouldn't I be?'

'Well, the second murder . . .'

'There's a feature of the homicide that makes DCS Bingham believe Carpenter could still be our killer,' Mike said. 'All will be revealed to you later today. Besides that, Carpenter's still on a drugs charge, remember. I need all the dirt I can get.' Mike looked about him. The corridor was too busy for what he wanted to say. 'Come out to the car park for a minute.'

It was raining. They stood under the roof overhang. Mike faced Chinnery squarely.

'I won't make this a drama unless you force me to. The woman you're seeing, Dorothy Beattie — I want you to pack it in. No tailing-off, not even an abrupt wind-up. Just don't go near her again.'

Chinnery stared at a puddle for a minute, his mouth puckered.

'It's a private matter, sir,' he said at last, not looking up. 'I keep it strictly separate from my work. I don't think you've the right to interfere.'

'I've taken it on myself to interfere,' Mike snapped, 'so that's that. Stop seeing her. It's an order.'

'I'm entitled to know why.'

'She's an undesirable.'

Chinnery looked up.

'Because she works in a nightclub?'

'No.'

'Why, then?'

Mike sighed.

'I want to know, sir.'

'She's a prostitute,' Mike said.

'That's rubbish!'

Mike grabbed the knot of Chinnery's tie. He pulled sharply then pushed. Chinnery would have fallen if Mike hadn't kept a grip.

'Don't you shout at me, buggerlugs. And don't question any statement I put forward as fact. Beattie is a brass, it's on record. If you were half a copper you'd have checked it out before you started laying pipe in dangerous swampland.' Mike released the tie and let Chinnery step back. 'Ladies like her can cancel a lot of old grudges if they get a copper to play with. Maybe she's wrecked your career already. Pray to God you're not the star of any infra-red Polaroids.'

Chinnery was staring at Mike but his mind was off elsewhere.

'I'm going for something to eat,' Mike said. 'I suggest you put new batteries in your pager then get back to the interview team. And Jim — don't go near her, all right? Not even to call her a cow.'

At twenty minutes past eight in the evening, Ross Carpenter was wheeled at speed on a trolley into the emergency room of the remand centre infirmary. He was transferred, protesting feebly, to a metal table where two prison officers held him down on his left side while a burly male nurse prepared to perform a stomach washout.

It was a protracted and distressing procedure, involving a long rubber tube which Carpenter had to swallow an inch at a time until one end was in his stomach. The other end was lowered to allow gastric fluid to trickle into a specimen bottle, then the washout commenced. Several gallons of warm water were passed into the stomach through the tube, a pint at a time, and siphoned out again until all traces of food and other matter had been eliminated. The tube was removed and Carpenter was given a thorough examination by a doctor. He was then transferred to a bed in the infirmary's medical ward.

At nine-fifteen he was visited by Kate Barbour, who was one of a group of practitioners — two psychiatrists, three physicians, three surgeons — who worked an evening rota for the prison service.

The officer guarding Carpenter withdrew to a discreet distance. Kate sat down by the bed. Her voice and expression were neutral as she introduced herself to Carpenter. He stared back at her sullenly, saying nothing.

'I'm here to determine why you took an overdose earlier this evening,' Kate said.

She studied Carpenter's face. He was built for belligerence, she decided, although tonight he was frightened. Fear seemed to scramble features like his, dismantling the hostility.

'It was a serious attempt, wasn't it? You weren't simply trying to draw attention to yourself, or to your predicament?'

Carpenter shifted his legs beneath the blankets. He sniffed loudly but still said nothing.

'How did you get hold of so many tablets?' Kate glanced at her notebook, open on her lap. 'They washed out thirty Taractan, fifty-mil strength. That's a serious drug, Ross. You certainly didn't have it on you when you were brought in here. Would you care to explain where it came from?'

She waited with no real expectation. Any prisoner who wanted drugs could get them, and none of them ever told how. Identifying the supplier would be no help in eliminating the source, anyway. A mystique surrounded the traffic. Whole blocks had been emptied in the past, the prisoners held in isolation while squads of officers combed the cells and cleared out every trace of drugs. The prisoners were subjected to an equally meticulous search-and-scour procedure before they were put back in their cells. Within days the dope traffic was as brisk as ever.

'Were you depressed?' Kate said. She waited, then added, 'Men on remand often get depressed.'

Men on remand often kill themselves.

Carpenter might have managed it if he hadn't choked on the second handful of tablets and began coughing so hard that an officer was alerted. Kate had noted that he was being held on suspicion of drug trafficking, and the chief officer had told her there was some suspicion among the police that Carpenter was implicated in another more serious case. No psychiatric profile was on record. Kate wondered if she should attempt one now. She changed her position on the chair, preparing to make a tentative start, then Carpenter spoke and made her forget about profiles.

'They're stitching me up,' he said, and there was a deep tremor in his voice. 'That fucking Fletcher and his boss.'

'Detective Inspector Fletcher, you mean?'

'Yeah, him. And Bingham. They don't want to know the truth. They just want me convicted.' Carpenter looked up from his tangled fingers and stared at Kate. 'They're going to do it.

They came into the remand wing and they sat there and they told me — I'm going down for two murders. Two!' Tears glinted at the corners of his eyes. 'I never murdered anybody in my fucking life!'

His shoulders heaved suddenly and he ducked his head, holding his breath, clenching his eyes shut to force back the tears. For nearly a minute he shook silently, his fists digging into the blanket.

'Policemen are good at bluffing,' Kate said. 'You should know that, you've tangled with them before.'

Carpenter took a deep shuddering breath, staring at her again.

'This was no bluff.'

'You can't be sure of that.'

'Yes I can! They're determined, those bastards. I could see it in their eyes. They told me how they're going to do it.'

'But they haven't charged you, have they?'

'A matter of time, that's all. They've got to get a killer. They don't like me, so I'm it. Christ.' A whimper escaped and he punched the bed. 'Somebody's got to help me. I've sod all to do with those murders.'

Kate studied his face again, saw him aching towards her now, beseeching. It had been a long time since she had seen someone so scared. She thought of Mike, realising there was a dimension to his nature he had kept hidden from her.

SEVENTEEN

DCS Derek Bingham met Mike Fletcher on the pavement in front of the police station a couple of minutes before 9 a.m. Bingham was on his way out of the building as Mike was going in. Raising his voice above the clamour of traffic noise, Bingham invited Mike to join him for breakfast.

They went to a quiet little all-day restaurant round the corner from the station. They ordered workmen's breakfasts and had large cups of coffee while they waited. Bingham broke part of the morning's baleful news.

'A special unit will be moving into the CID room first thing Monday morning. I'm on my way now for a briefing with the Deputy Chief Constable. As far as I'm aware, our visitors will be an eight-man team. You'll be asked to share a desk.'

'Terrific.'

'And of course, your full co-operation is expected. Commander Lithgow will brief you on how he expects you to behave.'

'I don't believe we've met.'

'Standard ex-MI5 type — approaches every problem with an open mouth.'

Mike glared at the window.

'I'm annoyed, too,' Bingham said. 'I don't think I'm going to take any of it lying down. I'm too old for subservience. On the other hand, I'm just the right age for a bit of subversion.'

'Anything in mind?'

'Nothing specific. It'll depend on how badly they get on my tits.' Bingham stared moodily across the restaurant. 'What grips me, I mean really *chokes* me, is the dishonesty of the

II2

exercise. I know perfectly well — and so do you — that as far as the case is concerned, these people will achieve nothing. We know, furthermore, that they don't *expect* to achieve anything. They function solely as a rebuke and a humiliation to real police officers. That's their job, the rest is frills. They're a governmental smack on the wrist.'

'Even so,' Mike said, 'it's a brave soul that tries to buck them. They can make life tough for mockers and dissenters.'

Bingham shrugged.

'I don't care about that.' He stared at Mike, measuring his reaction. 'I know you think I'm blowing hot air, but I mean it. I honestly don't give a monkey's what they're capable of doing.'

'Such recklessness.'

'It's just possible you're witnessing the emergence of the new me.' Bingham smiled, but there was a serious glint. 'I've been giving some thought to the quality of my existence. I reckon I'm unfulfilled.'

'This is what used to be called the midlife crisis, right?'

'Could be, but I suspect I'm just fed up distorting my nature to fit the job-definition.'

Mike promised he would steel himself for the changes.

'Do that. Watch out for the recreational aspects of my personality getting a lot more exercise.'

'I don't think I know what that means.'

'Well, to take an example, it's dawned on me that my sense of adventure can easily leapfrog my professional stability. So now and then I'm going to let it.'

'Sounds like fun.'

'You should know,' Bingham said.

Mike looked at him.

'You think I'm like that?'

'A lot of the time, yes.'

A little woman in black brought the breakfasts. As she set the plates in front of them Mike considered what the chief had said.

113

'No, it's different with me,' he said as the woman went away. 'I'm like a man who walks a tightrope not for a hobby or as a job, but because of a compulsion. I'm never really happy unless my balance is precarious.'

Bingham raised his knife and fork and held them above his plate.

'OK,' he said, 'I'll grant you there's a *slight* difference there. But can we agree that we both tend to enjoy situations that put us at risk?'

'Oh, sure.'

'Right. So if I make an occasional prat of myself, I can rely on at least one person to understand.'

Bingham lowered his cutlery. They began to eat.

The food was delicious. The eggs — they had two each — had been deep-fried and were globe shaped, the whites wrapped around the hot soft yolks like cocoons. Because the bacon had been cured in the old-fashioned way — with block salt instead of injected saline — it was crisp and aromatic. The mushrooms and fried bread presented exquisite contrasts of texture and flavour. Bingham dropped a few remarks about murderous fat levels, but his plate was cleared before Mike's.

When the woman came to tidy away, Bingham ordered more coffee. Then he broke the rest of the news.

'Carpenter tried to top himself last night. An overdose. They got to him in plenty of time, though. Pumped him out.'

Mike waited.

'Apparently he told a doctor he did it because he was being pressured and threatened about a couple of murders he didn't commit.'

'That's bloody awful,' Mike said. 'I never believed he was guilty in the first place. This didn't need to happen.'

'Guilty men try to kill themselves too,' Bingham said.

'You don't *still* think it might be him?'

'I haven't abandoned the suspicion. His suicide attempt is an aggravation — we'll have to handle him more carefully in future — but it doesn't change anything, as far as I can see.'

Mike would have argued, but at that moment his pager sounded. He went to the pay phone and called the station desk. The sergeant said a girl was waiting to see him. She said it was very important and the sergeant believed her. Mike said he would be there in three minutes.

The girl had been taken to an interview room. When Mike went in she was sitting at the table hand-rolling a cigarette. She was about twenty, tall and a fraction too thin. She had pale downy skin and her bleached hair was cropped short in an attempt at an Annie Lennox look. When she glanced up at Mike he was reminded of the ridiculously innocent eyes of a lemur. She wore a T-shirt with a picture of Van Morrison, a fluorescent blue miniskirt and PVC knee boots.

'Good morning,' Mike said brightly. He closed the door. 'I'm Detective Inspector Fletcher.' He came and sat opposite her. 'How can I help you, Miss . . . '

'Wallis,' she said. 'Sophie Wallis.' She held up the cigarette. 'All right to smoke this in here?'

'Of course.'

Mike gave her a light and watched her take a leisurely puff. He sniffed carefully, from habit. It was Old Holborn.

'I read your name in the paper,' Sophie said. 'For a while I didn't know what I should do, then I decided I better come and see you.'

Mike noticed now how nervous she was. The cigarette trembled between her fingers and her voice had a shaky undertow. She was trying to look cool and in control of herself.

'It's to do with the murder . . . '

Mike's attention picked up.

'Which one?'

'Well . . . '

He watched her straighten, surer of herself now she was committed. She cleared her throat.

'Both of them, really.'

She took a puff on the cigarette. Mike felt a sharp urge to snatch it out of her hand.

'So? Do you know something?'

'I knew both the men.'

There had been plenty of people who 'knew' the dead men. Dozens had been interviewed. They all knew just about the same, which in terms of investigational usefulness was practically nothing.

'Did they know *you* at all, Sophie?'

She scowled at Mike, as if she found the question flippant.

'Of course they did. We were friends.'

'Then why didn't you get in touch before?'

The hand with the cigarette scratched the back of the other hand.

'When they both went missing that weekend, and then Jishrah turned up murdered, I didn't know what to do.'

'I don't follow.'

Sophie took a couple of quick puffs, frowning.

'I haven't explained it right,' she said. 'I was Ahmed's girlfriend. I knew them both, but it was Ahmed I went out with. You can see what I mean, the problem I had, right? When they found Jishrah dead, I couldn't help wondering if Ahmed had anything to do with it. He was still missing, after all . . .'

Mike was nodding.

'So you kept quiet. Then you heard about Ahmed being found murdered, just like Jishrah.'

'Right. But even then I wasn't sure what to do.'

'Why was that?'

'My family. Well, my parents, anyway. They'd hit the bloody roof if they knew I'd been seeing a coloured bloke. They're backward about things like that.' She paused and pointed her cigarette at Mike for an instant. 'That's what I meant to say already — my folks won't have to know about this, will they?'

Mike performed the customary sharp intake of breath.

'It'd be hard to keep them in the dark. I mean, we couldn't actually go round and tell them about you helping us with the case, but if this comes to anything positive, there's other ways they're bound to find out.'

Sophie was quiet for a minute.

'Sod it, then,' she said at last. 'I'm browned off living at home anyway. If they start on at me, I'll clear off out of it.'

'So,' Mike said, 'what made you decide to come and speak to me, in spite of the trouble you could make for yourself?'

'I thought it was important. I still think it is. See, the Friday night Ahmed and Jishrah went missing, I knew what they were up to — what they were going to do, like.'

Mike waited, scarcely breathing, while she had another puff.

'They were going to the Buck and Ferret to score some hash.'

She stopped and frowned at Mike.

Is that it? he thought.

'I can't get done for this, can I?' she said.

'For what?'

'Admitting I knew somebody was scoring dope?'

'No, no, don't worry about that.' Mike's heart had dropped several inches, or so it felt. 'You know who they were going to buy it from, I suppose?'

'Carpenter. They always scored off him.'

Another confirmation. As if he needed any. But there could still be a breakthrough, Mike told himself. Settle her down with coffee and more cigarettes, get her talking about old times — it was surprising what could turn up in casual recollection.

'After that,' Sophie said, 'they were going to pick up forged papers.'

Mike stared at her.

'They what?'

'It was arranged a week or so before. It was going to cost them a packet but Ahmed reckoned it was worth it.'

'When you say forged papers — '

'Passports. Immigration documents. Things like that.'

'For both of them?'

117

'Sure.'

So Ahmed Faiz was an illegal, too. The computers hadn't come up with that yet.

'Do you know where they were going to get the documents?'

Sophie shook her head.

'They were very secretive about it, you know? Sworn to secrecy, that's how Ahmed put it. He said it was because the identity and whereabouts of the supplier had to be protected, and if they blabbed they wouldn't get their papers and might get a duffing into the bargain.'

Mike nodded glumly.

'But I got his name, all the same,' Sophie said.

'The supplier?'

'Yeah. I listened a couple of times when the lads got pissed, when they thought they were talking all quiet and secret. They were dead odd like that, they'd always talk louder when they were pissed or stoned, yet they'd think — '

'The name,' Mike snapped, aware he was letting the professionalism slip. 'What was the name?'

'Sittim, Mr Sittim, that's what they called him. They contacted him through some Asian bigwig — an illegal immigrant himself, I think. They didn't drop his name.'

Mike sat back, drumming the table with one hand.

'Can you spare me an hour or so, Sophie? I want to go over this in more detail with you and get it written down.'

'Yeah, no sweat.'

'I'll organise coffee and biscuits. Won't be a minute.'

Mike stood up. He would get the man's name searched while he interviewed Sophie. With luck and some smart elimination, he could have a result before the day was out.

He looked at her again, submitting to a small worry.

'Sophie, I couldn't help noticing something. You told me Ahmed Faiz was your boyfriend.'

'Well? He was.'

'You don't seem all that upset that he's dead.'

Sophie ground out her tiny cigarette end in the tinfoil ashtray.

'I was upset at the time I heard,' she said. 'But I can't say I'm broken-hearted or anything like that. It wasn't a *love* thing between us. He needed a girl to hang around with him — you know, to show off and take to the pubs and clubs, and for the occasional bit of you-know-what. I needed somebody to take me places and buy me the things I couldn't afford. The arrangement suited us both. I'm sorry about what happened, but it's not as if we were *attached*. Not in a real sense, know what I mean?'

'Sure, of course,' Mike said, feeling his age.

EIGHTEEEN

Since the previous afternoon nothing had looked the same to Jim Chinnery. He felt like a man viewing his life and his surroundings from a new and curious angle. Sights and sounds, colours and perspectives were changed and discordant. Harmony was lost.

He knew what was wrong. The same had happened to him when his mother died. His doctor had put it on the sick note: *mental disorientation arising from profound emotional shock*. It would be days before the familiar looked familiar again, maybe weeks before his mind could abandon its repetitive scans of bruising memory.

Revels seemed different, too. He had been there in daylight before, but it hadn't looked this way — though part of the reason could be because it was so early. Beams of dusty light poked down into the bar from open fanlights. Smoke with no visible source drifted in a flat cloud over the bar top. Chinnery stared at the bottles and optics on the back fitting and didn't find them familiar. He felt as if he were entering the place for the first time, finding his way from the recollection of an inaccurate picture.

There was no one about. He leaned on the bar and closed his eyes, momentarily giving in to the pain in his head. The night before he hardly slept, and when he did the dreams were terrible. For maybe twenty seconds when he woke up he was all right, he felt fine, but then he remembered and let out an involuntary groan. By the time he was washed and dressed he had known there was no way to stop himself coming here.

'We're not open yet, squire.'

The man who had appeared behind the bar was Jerry Grice. Chinnery knew it even though he had never met him before. Sleaze incarnate, that was DI Fletcher's description. Grice was big, bordering on fat, his stomach sucked in under a yellow silk shirt. He had unnaturally black hair and hooded brown eyes. His mouth looked unpleasantly wet.

'I wondered if I might have a word with Dorothy Beattie,' Chinnery said.

'I told you, we're not open yet.'

'I'm a police officer.'

Grice remained where he was, blinking at Chinnery.

'No trouble, I hope.'

'No, no.' Chinnery forced a smile. 'It's just a little matter that concerns her. Nothing to worry about.'

Grice took a step back and pointed to the office.

'She's in there.'

Jim went round the bar and tapped on the office door. There was no response but he went in anyway, feeling Grice's eyes on his back.

Dorothy looked up from a newspaper spread open on the desk. Chinnery's expression warned her about something.

'You're early,' she said brightly. 'Fancy a cup of coffee?'

He shook his head.

'I came because there's something I need to know.'

Seeing Dorothy now in brisk daylight, he couldn't hold back a memory of her in the half dark. She sat erect now, her back and shoulders tensed, ready for the trouble he was signalling.

'Don't get angry with me,' he croaked. 'Just answer my question . . . '

Once, life had been simple and humdrum. He wished with painful intensity that it could be like that now. But how could it? He licked his lips and dredged up his voice again.

'Do you see other men?'

Dorothy frowned incomprehension.

'*See* other men? What are you getting at, Jimmy?'

121

A further hurt. She took him for a fool. Her puzzlement was a transparent sham, the kind that only berks and wallies fell for. As far as she was concerned he was one of their number — otherwise she would have tried harder.

'I'm asking you if you're intimate with other men.'

Dorothy ran her tongue in a swift circle inside her cheek.

'You mean do I fuck other men?'

The harshness shocked him. Her voice had scraped the air. He swallowed hard.

'What's the readout on this, Jim? Who's stirring the shit?'

'That doesn't matter.'

'To *me* it matters!'

'I've — ' He stopped and started again. 'It's been suggested to me that you're a prostitute.'

'Oh my. It's been *suggested*, has it? It'll be *allegations*, next. This is serious stuff.' She made it sound jokey but her eyes were furious. 'Maybe I should get myself a brief. Would you recommend that, officer?'

'Is it true, Dorothy? I know you've a record — '

'Oh, I'll bet you know!'

'The past doesn't concern me,' Chinnery said. 'It's now I want to know about.'

'You sound pathetic, do you know that?'

'Dorothy — '

'Why do you need to know this? Can't you be content with things as they are? What's so bad about a bit of fun on the side, with no strings?'

'It meant more than that to me,' he said.

'Well it didn't to me, whatever you might have let yourself imagine.'

It was like being wounded, he thought.

'*Do* you have other men?'

'I'm telling you nothing.' Dorothy stood up and came around the desk. 'I've no more to say to you, so if you'll excuse me, there's work to be done.'

She made to brush past him and he caught her by the arm.

122

The contact was unsettling. The feel of her flesh was something he could imagine lucidly, but now there was no compliance in her and his disorientation deepened. She felt entirely changed, another woman.

'Let go, you bastard!'

'Please, listen to me — '

She wriggled to free herself. Chinnery tightened his grip and an image flared: Dorothy naked on the bed, face down, feet spread, creamy buttocks undulating as she implored him . . .

'Let me bloody *go*!'

The door was flung open and Grice stood there. He watched Dorothy detach herself from Chinnery's slackened grip.

'Why do I get the feeling this isn't business?'

'He's just going,' Dorothy said, glaring at Chinnery.

He stared back at her. He was appalled by the situation. This woman who had totally captivated him, who had made profound changes in his mind and pesonality, was now dismissing him. It could be too much to bear.

'Well don't just stand there,' Grice said, moving back from the doorway.

Chinnery took a step forward then stopped. He looked at Dorothy again.

'I don't want to leave it like this.'

'You've no choice,' she said.

The rejection was absolute. And even if she hadn't rejected him there would still be the gut-twisting truth she wouldn't admit, the indelible fact that for money, other men were admitted to her body. The thought was unbearable and as he flinched from it a question throbbed forward: all that eagerness and hot ingenuity — had it been real, or was it the same counterfeit she plied to her customers, a performance from a gifted professional?

Chinnery looked at Grice.

'Leave us alone for a while, will you?'

'Your time's up, pal.' Grice jerked a thumb over his shoulder. 'Out. Now.'

'Five minutes, it's all I'm asking.' Chinnery heard the pleading in his voice. It was hateful but he couldn't help it. He looked at Dorothy and saw how she despised him now. 'Come out with me for a coffee,' he said. 'So we can talk. I can't just walk away, and I can't let you do it either.'

'It's all over,' Dorothy said. 'Get that fixed in your head. It was no big deal anyway.'

The change in her was heartbreaking.

'Will you come with me? Coffee, only a few minutes . . .'

Dorothy looked at Grice, who was still hovering. Her eyes narrowed as she turned them to Chinnery again.

'If you don't go now, I'll ring the station and lay a complaint. I'll say you assaulted me.'

'And in the meantime,' Grice said, 'I'll have the pleasure of kicking you arse-over-appetite for laying hands on one of my employees.'

'Don't threaten me,' Chinnery said. He turned on Grice and felt a segment of the pain convert to anger. 'One finger on me gets your whole arm broken.' He looked beyond Grice and saw a young woman watching them. 'I think somebody wants to see you.'

Grice turned, glared at the girl.

'Wait in my office, Cora,' he snapped.

She went away. Grice turned back to confront Chinnery, but he wasn't facing him any more. He was standing directly in front of Dorothy Beattie, looking down at her.

'This has shattered me,' he said.

Mangled emotions squirmed in him. He stared hard at Dorothy, making himself see her as she was: cold, hostile, an enemy. She was the source of his hurt, he had to believe that and hold to it. With a tremendous effort he began focusing blame.

'I think it'll be a long time before I feel any better,' he said. 'But I'm glad I came here and let you put me through this. Now I can be determined about something.'

'And what's that?' Dorothy demanded, curious in spite of herself.

124

'I'm going to make myself hate you. I can't do it just yet, but I will. Then I'll start keeping an eye on you. A policeman's eye. One day you'll make a wrong move and I'll find a way to make you feel as bad as I do right now. Don't take that lightly, because I mean it. Every copper's got a long-term target. You're going to be mine.'

When he left the club he drove directly to the station and managed to find a space in the car park. For a while he stayed behind the wheel, feeling the aches clamouring for attention. There was a tiny consolation, he supposed, in knowing his threat had shaken Dorothy badly. He had no intention of targeting her, but she would never know that. He saw her scowling face again and winced.

I have to get over all this.

Cure would be a matter of stiff-necked resolve and intense diversion. He must also keep reminding himself how Dorothy had behaved today, and *never* think about the hours he spent alone with her.

He stared dolefully at the back of the station. He wasn't suicidal, so he *would* mend. What was important now was to establish a time for the process of healing to begin, for he knew it was psychologically important to have a precise onset.

He would give it an hour. Sixty minutes wallowing in regret and self-pity, then *ping*! he would tell himself he was starting to mend. He checked his watch, set the alarm and decided to have coffee.

On the way to the canteen something edged in on his gloom. At first he couldn't make out what it was. Something at the club . . .

It was the girl. Grice called her Cora. She would be Cora Oswyn, the one he planned to interview today or at latest tomorrow. He pictured her and something else began to bother him. He concentrated. Nothing came.

In the canteen he got on the end of the coffee queue. Somebody spoke to him and he stared back, distracted. When the woman at the urns asked him if he wanted a large coffee or a small one, there was a five second pause before he answered. At the till he put the cashier in a mood by handing her a ten-pound note.

He took his coffee to a corner table and sat with his hands round the cup, gazing at nothing. Whatever it was, the unspecified something about Cora Oswyn, he felt it should be ringing an alarm.

What the hell was it?

He sighed and sipped his coffee, unaware that the puzzle was giving his brain a rest from Dorothy Beattie.

NINETEEN

'So what brings you here?' Mike said.

Kate Barbour waved her hand at the row of pump handles.

'My love of English ale, I suppose.'

He had been startled to find her sitting at the bar in the Grampian.

'I've been across the road at the mortuary,' he said. 'I was having another look at the second body. Hunting for inspiration. Now tell me — what really brought you here?'

'The near-certainty that this is where I'd find you at this time today. You're a creature of habit, whether you know it or not.'

'I know it. I try to cover the signs.'

Mike leaned on the bar and found himself momentarily overwhelmed by her perfume. He had forgotten its keen familiarity.

'So you wanted to talk,' he said. 'Can I say, right away, that I'm sorry for the way I spoke to you on the phone? I felt vulnerable. I think I over-reacted to *your* over-reaction.'

A second before Kate spoke, he saw the tautening of the skin under her eyes and knew she was here to make another bombing run.

'Did you know I interviewed Ross Carpenter after he tried to kill himself?' She put her head delicately on one side. 'Have you seen him yourself since then, I wonder?'

'No, and no.'

'You should get over there as soon as you can. Have a gloat while the terror's fresh.'

'I think I've caught this act before,' Mike said. 'What's

happened to you? Why this emotional turnaround where I'm concerned? Why the compulsion to chase me up and stick the boot in?'

'Don't ascribe this encounter to any problem in my private life,' Kate said haughtily. She leaned close and tapped the bar with a stiffened finger. 'You and your chief systematically terrorised a suspect. That's the issue here.'

'We didn't terrorise anybody.'

'You *did*. I've listened to the tape. I've seen the wreckage of the prisoner. You used levels of menace and threat that went miles beyond the humane boundaries.'

'What humane boundaries are you talking about, Doctor?'

'The ones laid down in international agreements concerning the treatment of prisoners in police custody — you *know* the boundaries I mean.'

'They're not statutory. They're only recommendations.'

'It's the principle that matters,' Kate hissed. 'You leaned on Carpenter ferociously. He was scared into unreason and in that state he made an authentic attempt to kill himself.'

'That's your way of looking at it.'

'Of course it is. It's the correct way. And you should be punished for doing something like that. It's barbaric.'

Mike looked around. People were listening again. Kate's voice carried like a bell across water.

'Carpenter isn't a nice man,' Mike said quietly.

'That's no excuse for what — '

'Ssh. Listen to me for a minute. He's a very unpleasant piece of work. He has no scruples, or none we can discover. He's a drug pedlar, an active racist, something of a sadist. A real shit. Do you expect me to kid myself this is a decent human being who finds himself temporarily fallen from grace? He's not a man to reason with, Kate. With the likes of Carpenter you don't coax or cajole.'

'Of course not,' Kate said flatly. 'You badger and harangue them until they're half mad with fright and want to kill themselves.'

128

'Do you really think we'd do that deliberately?'

Kate clasped her hands and examined the nails.

'No, I don't think that. It's not what I was saying, anyway.'

'At this point I'll make a small confession,' Mike said. 'When I heard he'd taken an overdose I was upset — and not because I was worried I'd be reprimanded. I was upset because I'd never wanted to pressure Carpenter that way in the first place.'

'Are you blaming Bingham for making you do it?'

'No. I blame myself for agreeing to go along with his idea. The only glimmer of justification I can offer is that we were in a very tight corner. The circumstances were unusual, and they continue that way.'

'What's up?'

Mike glanced at her. A beam of her familiar self had slipped through.

'We're about to be overridden,' he said. 'Supplanted. Temporarily of course, but things'll never be the same. Internal procedures will be seriously undermined. Lovingly built networks will get wrecked. Relationships with certain public sectors will be shredded.'

'Because you've got nobody for these murders?'

Mike nodded.

'It doesn't excuse you trying to frighten Carpenter into a confession, does it?'

'DCS Bingham genuinely believed Carpenter was a probable.'

'Does he still believe it?'

'I don't really know.'

'And you?'

'I never confidently believed he was even a likely,' Mike said.

Tacitly, with a small change in the level of her voice, Kate abandoned the reproach.

'So what'll happen to Carpenter now?'

'Oh . . . ' Mike shrugged. 'Special squad officers will talk to him. Like me they'll decide he's got only a loose circumstantial connection to the case. He'll go to court on drugs charges, nothing else.'

They were quiet for a minute.

'I've been missing us,' Mike said.

Kate moved her shoulders in a way that committed her to no view of the matter, although the gesture didn't look unfriendly.

'Life's certainly quieter,' she said at last.

They permitted themselves another careful silence.

'Maybe it's better that way,' Mike said slowly, 'until we stop having such expectations of each other.'

She frowned at that.

'Kate — did you really come here today just to give me a bollocking?'

'No,' she said, and now her voice scarcely carried at all. 'I wanted to see you. Just to see you.' She wasn't smiling. The explanation seemed to trouble her. She frowned a little more. 'I did feel strongly about Carpenter, of course . . .'

'And he was an excuse for you to bawl me out. Again.'

Kate went on frowning.

'What did you mean just now, about us having such expectations of each other?'

'People aren't consistent, even from hour to hour. How can you have firm expectations?'

Kate stared at her drink for a moment.

'There are a lot of psychological niggles I could trot out, but I haven't the energy.'

'Too early in the day to take it any further, anyway,' Mike said. 'I need brandy to get my head seriously round that kind of stuff. All I'm saying is, our expectations of each other are maybe too precise, for whatever reason. Too rigid.'

'That could be true,' Kate said. 'But I also think it's hard to stop doing it.'

'Can I suggest something?'

'Could I stop you?'

'Let's play it by ear. I mean *really*, with no calculation. No copper's cunning on my side, no shrink tactics on yours. The way we were in the beginning.'

'We were a fall-about act in the early days,' Kate pointed out.

'So? Are we too old for that now?'

'Perhaps not. But maybe we know each other too well to be spontaneous any more.'

'Kate.' Mike beckoned her with a waggling finger. She leaned close. 'Cobblers,' he whispered, and stepped back. 'Now. This is ungracious of me and you'll probably call me every shade of blackguard, but I've got to go.'

'Really? No time for just one more drink?'

It was minor bliss to hear Kate sound like herself again.

'A quick one, then. Just at the moment I'm staying on top of the troops. I'm chasing a hope that I can get a lead running and pull us out of the poo before the faceless ones move in.'

'Anything to go on?'

'A name. I thought it would connect straight away, but so far we've come up with zilch.'

He emptied his glass and ordered two more drinks.

'As soon as this case is over, we can have a proper get-together,' Kate said. 'Clear the air, all that stuff.'

'A grand idea. And for a while at least, we won't approach the subject of living together.' Mike watched her frown again. 'I'm not ready for playing house, not full time. I will be. But not yet. Can you believe that?'

Kate promised, not quite huffily, that she would try.

At four o'clock DCS Bingham hailed Mike in the corridor outside the CID room. He brandished a single sheet of computer paper.

'Here's the news, for what it's worth.'

He handed over the search results on Sittim, the name of the alleged supplier of papers to illegal immigrants. Only three name-matches had been found among Asians in the city. Two of them were a married couple, neither very bright, known to be illiterate and generally feckless. The third was a frail eighty-six-year-old who had not left his home for more than a year.

'Of course we only have his neighbours' word that he's decrepit,' Bingham said. 'Could be a character-acting job, couldn't it?'

The reference was to a young rapist, an actor, who had stalked his victims across the city disguised as an old man.

A five-line extract from a Department of Immigration register showed that, in a twenty-year period, seventy-eight immigrant Asians from the city had been investigated on suspicion of possessing falsified personal documentation. They had all appeared before the Department's interrogation panel; more than half their number were subsequently deported to their country of origin. One of those investigated and questioned had been Mani Chandra. It was noted that no action had been taken against him, though his record now carried a 'suspect' tag. The suspicion arose from the fact that Chandra's history and records were impeccable: in the view of the Department that was simply impossible, given that the man was engaged in the import trade.

'It backs up what I've always thought,' Mike said. 'The cleaner you are, the more dirty speculation you attract.'

There was a summary paragraph about a parallel check run on known forgers of official documents — paper men, as they were called. Supplies within the city of suitable paper and ink had shrunk in recent years, and the penalties for counterfeiting under the 1981 Forgery and Counterfeiting Act had discouraged most of the old hands. Four former outlets and three possible new ones had been combed and the operators — jobbing printers — thoroughly questioned. Old forgers known to be sporadically active had been vigorously grilled; snouts had been questioned. The consensus was that no new paper had been on the move in the city for months.

'I think we might as well clear space in our desks and get ready for the inevitable, Mike.'

Bingham was on the point of suggesting a crafty drink when DC Chinnery came running through the swing doors at the end of the corridor. When he saw Mike Fletcher he started waving.

'I wonder if this is good tidings, or another disaster,' Bingham murmured.

Chinnery drew up beside them, panting.

'Glad I caught you sir,' he said, addressing Mike. He paused to catch his breath. 'All day something's been bugging me. Something about that woman from Revels, Cora Oswyn — '

'You interviewed her, then?'

'No sir, not yet. But I saw her this morning, very briefly. Afterwards I kept feeling there was something about her that should have got me on the alert — something familiar, maybe.'

'So?' Bingham demanded. 'What was it? More to the point, does it help the case at all?'

'It wasn't anything familiar,' Chinnery said. 'It was that thing you mentioned, sir — the fish ornament, remember?'

'Gopal's, you mean?' Mike nodded. 'Of course I remember.'

'Well, Cora Oswyn was wearing one this morning. Silver, shaped like a fish, with Indian lettering on the side.'

'When did this dawn on you?'

'Two minutes ago.'

'Right. Let's go and find Cora Oswyn.' Mike looked at Bingham. 'Coming, sir?'

'No,' Bingham said, 'I'll stay here and mind the shop, like a good DCS. I'll be waiting for an update, remember. Make it something encouraging, chaps. I deserve it.'

TWENTY

The day had been studded with aggravations. After the ruction with the cop in the morning there was a mix-up with spirit deliveries — two cases of gin instead of three of whisky — that nearly led to punches being thrown. At midday there was a tussle with a big drunk punter who insisted he had been short-changed, and smashed a Guinness pump with a soda siphon when the girl on the bar denied it. Tony Webb, the assistant manager, twisted his back throwing the man out; at the emergency unit they gave Webb a bottle of pain killers and told him to stay in bed for at least a week. Three more malcontents materialised during the evening session: one tried to start a fire in the toilets and the other two turned the jukebox on its face. At ten past three Jerry Grice decided to call it a night. He locked the door behind the last straggler and invited Dorothy Beattie to join him for a drink.

They went to his office. Ostentation and poor taste gave the room the appearance of an overstocked Sixties boutique. One wall was completely covered with alternated bronze and green mirror panels. A life-size aluminium female nude served as a coat stand. Long black sideboards stood against three walls: two were decked with chrome-wire mobiles, statuettes of old-time film stars and framed, autographed pictures of naked and semi-naked women — Grice 'collected' strippers. The third sideboard was cluttered with wine and spirit bottles, elaborately engraved crystal glasses and a vase full of customised drink-stirrers collected from clubs and bars all over Britain.

Dorothy said she would like a scotch. Grice gave her a large one and poured a brandy for himself.

'Take the weight off,' he said. 'You must be as knackered as I am.'

They sat at opposite sides of the desk, a massive burled-walnut piece Grice had acquired in lieu of a debt.

'What's the take looking like?' It was nearly always his first question at the end of the day. 'Ignoring deductions for damages,' he added sourly.

'Two hundred and ninety-three up on this time last week,' Dorothy said.

Grice made an approving sound. He ran his tongue along his already wet lips and took a gulp of brandy.

'It makes the aggro easier to take when you know your popularity's going up. That's a steady climb eight weeks on the trot.' He winked at Dorothy. 'We're keeping the fox from the cocktail cabinet, one way and another.'

Dorothy smiled coolly, took a sip of her drink. Grice pulled a note pad across the desk and squinted at it.

'I took a pencilling for you on the phone,' he said. 'Mr Armstrong. Estate agent. Remember him?'

Dorothy nodded again.

'Monday afternoon. Can you accommodate?'

'Sure.'

'I'll get back to him in the morning and confirm. Two o'clock, Raglan Hotel, the usual.' Grice looked up from the pad. 'What *is* the usual with him?'

'Armstrong . . . ' Dorothy put her head back for a minute, thinking. 'Oh, yes. He varied it a bit, until he was able to say what he really wanted. He's an easy number — kneels in front of the loo, lets me put handcuffs on him, then I force him down and flush the pan in his face.'

Grice looked coldly amused.

'He's happy to cough up seventy-five for that?'

'I'm expected to turn in a good performance with the domination bit,' Dorothy said. 'And he likes a rubber handjob for finishers.'

'Even so, it's decent bunce for ten minutes graft with no

hassle.' Grice leaned back, sniffing at the rim of his glass, watching Dorothy. 'What's eating you?'

'Sorry?'

'Don't come it. You've got something on your mind. You've been as vague as a pipe-head all night.'

'I'm just tired.'

'I know what you look like when you're tired. It's different from how you look tonight.'

Dorothy clucked, stared at the drinks sideboard for a second.

'It's Jim Chinnery, I suppose. I can't get it out of my head, what he said . . . '

'What — about making you a target?' Grice twisted his mouth. 'That was bullshit. He had to say *something*, didn't he?'

'It sounded to me like he meant it.'

'He was just sore, it'll wear off.'

'I've had trouble before.'

'Yeah, so? Who hasn't?'

'That lunatic Briggs. He was a lot like Chinnery, in looks and temperament. He threatened to kill me, right?'

'But he didn't kill you.'

'He tried, Jerry.'

'Half-hearted stuff.' Grice flapped his hand dismissively. 'We stopped him because he wanted to get stopped.'

'This is different. Chinnery's a cop.'

'No difference at all. He's been led by the dick. The ones that let that happen are all the same underneath.'

Dorothy shrugged one shoulder and drank more whisky.

'What did you see in that dumb fuck anyway?'

'Nothing I can explain.'

'You're right about him and Briggs being the same. A matching pair of arseholes.' Grice shook his head. 'I never interfered in your recreational side, but at times I've wondered if being on the game's knocked something loose in your skull.'

'There's no accounting for taste, remember,' Dorothy said. 'I see a certain type of man and I go all funny. Even if he's something dodgy.'

'Like a cop.'

'Yeah.'

'And you don't know why.'

'Maybe I'm self-destructive,' Dorothy said, a little too sharply.

She was never inclined to question her impulses where men were concerned. When she wanted someone she went after him. It was recreational, as Grice said, an exciting game. The problem with certain of the men who drew her, shy married types like the engineer Briggs and the policeman Chinnery — men who, above all, could be *lured* — was their tendency to be possessive.

'I think we should both be worried about Chinnery,' she said now. 'He asked questions about you a couple of times.'

'What kind of questions?'

'Nothing direct — just general stuff. I don't think he knows much, but him and his cronies have got our bouncer banged up, haven't they? They're bound to grill him about what goes on here, and — '

'And now Chinnery's got a bit of extra incentive to find things out.'

'Uh-huh.'

'Point taken.'

Grice sat forward in his chair. He gulped the remainder of his brandy and looked at Dorothy through watery eyes.

'You're a good girl. One of the best. I won't hear a word against you. But . . . ' He let out a slow sigh. 'I do wish to Christ you had better taste in men. Apart from anything else, it'd save *me* a pile of trouble, wouldn't it?'

Cora Oswyn rounded the corner at the top of the stairs and stopped so fast her heels skidded. She looked at the two men leaning on the wall beside her front door. One of them she recognised, but she couldn't think from where.

'Miss Oswyn?' Mike Fletcher stepped forward. 'We've been trying to get hold of you since yesterday afternoon.' He showed her his warrant card and introduced himself. 'You've been away, I take it.'

'I was staying with a friend.' Cora dug out her keys from a big white handbag and stood rattling them. She made no move to open the door. 'What can I do for you, Inspector?'

'Can we come in and talk?'

'I'm not sure about that . . . '

Mike watched her as she scanned the windows of the surrounding flats. She was tall and full in the figure, a tight-lipped girl with big blue-green eyes set rather too far apart. Her shiny brown hair was just long enough to touch her shoulders.

'I've got to watch it with the neighbours,' she said. 'I mean, two men coming inside with me in broad daylight — I can just imagine what these mucky old buggers would think. They'd complain to the council, too, don't imagine they wouldn't. Complaining's the only fun they get.'

'Inside would be better than standing out here,' Mike insisted.

Cora stared at him, like someone waiting for a reprieve. He stared back.

'Suit yourself,' she said finally. 'I don't suppose I'm in a position to argue, anyway.' She unlocked the door and led the way inside. 'Mind your heads on the wind chimes.'

The living room was tidy and quietly furnished. The carpet was brown and beige; a peppering of glittery highlights betrayed its nylon content. There was a three-piece suite covered in brown and dark-yellow print fabric with a floral design, and a matching pouffe. A bamboo-legged glass coffee table sat in front of the couch. In the magazine rack, bamboo again, a copy of *Vogue* stuck up pretentiously among several issues of *Woman's Own*. A reproduction seascape hung above the tiled fireplace.

'We'll get right to the point,' Mike said, declining a chair. 'You have a pendant, a silver one shaped like a fish, that you wear on a chain round your neck, right?'

For the tiniest instant Cora's face was guarded, then she stared blankly.

'You do have an ornament like that, don't you?'

'It's news to me,' she said.

'I saw you wearing it yesterday, love,' Chinnery said.

'No you didn't.' Cora shook her head at both of them. 'You've made a mistake. I'd know if I had something like that, wouldn't I?'

'Yes, I believe you would,' Mike said. 'Now can we stop messing about, please? You have the ornament. We want to see it and we want to know where you got it. The matter isn't trivial, Miss Oswyn. We're investigating a serious crime.'

'Crime?' Now she tried to look helpless. 'Jesus. What do you want me to do? I can't conjure the thing up, just because you want it to be here.'

'Right, that's enough,' Mike said.

He stamped across to the living room door.

'Where are you going?' Cora demanded.

'To the bedroom, for starters. DC Chinnery can search in here.'

'Wait,' Cora said.

They waited.

'It's in the box on the window ledge.'

Chinnery went to the side window and opened a wooden cigar box. It was crammed with brooches, rings and necklaces. He picked up the fish ornament, teasing the chain out between the other pieces. He brought it to Mike.

'Fine. We're getting somewhere.' Mike fingered the little effigy, seeing it glint as he flexed its hinges. 'Now tell us where you got it.'

'It was a present.'

'From?'

'I don't remember.'

'Miss Oswyn, please . . .'

'It was a long time ago,' she protested. 'I know a lot of

people. They're always giving me jewellery — that box is full of it.'

Mike pressed on the underside of the pendant. The head clicked softly and flipped back. He looked at Cora.

'Did you know it could do that?'

She gaped at it.

'I — no, no I didn't.'

She watched as Mike tipped the fish on end and shook it. A small brown lump fell out on his palm.

'And of course you didn't know that was inside.'

They looked at each other. Cora's face was turning pink.

'You know what it is, don't you?' Mike held the lump up in front of her, close to her nose. 'About a quarter ounce there, I reckon. Top quality cannabis.'

'It's not mine,' Cora snapped.

'It probably belonged to whoever gave you the ornament. And I suppose you still can't remember who that was.'

The room went silent. The detectives stared and Cora tried not to flinch.

'We have to assume,' Mike said quietly, 'that since the cannabis was found in your possession, it's yours. It could mean you get charged, if you don't choose to recall where the pendant came from.'

'I told you already,' Cora said, not looking at either of them. 'I don't remember who gave me that thing.'

Mike decided that isolation from familiar surroundings might slacken her stubbornness. He dropped the fish into his pocket, scooping in the loops of chain on top of it.

'I think we should retire to the station and do the rest of our talking there,' he said.

'What for?' Cora looked startled. 'What do we need to go there for?'

Mike picked up her jacket and handed it to her.

'There's a lot more than the pendant and the cannabis to talk about,' he said, leading the way out to the hall. 'There's your relationship with Ross Carpenter, for one

140

thing. And I'd like to know about the work you do for Jerry Grice.'

He opened the front door and stepped out on to the landing. Cora followed him, with Chinnery on her heels.

'Having all that to discuss,' Mike said, watching Cora lock the door, 'we might as well be where there's a good supply of coffee on tap.'

Cora said nothing. She turned and marched stiffly down the stairs.

TWENTY-ONE

The infirmary was gloomy, the daylight appearing to fade just inside the high barred windows. Carpenter was drowsing in a chair at the side of the bed. He wore a fawn corduroy prison-issue dressing gown and brown checked slippers. He woke with a jump as Mike Fletcher dropped a drawing pad on his lap.

'Sorry to hear you've been poorly, Ross.'

Carpenter rubbed his eyes with flattened fingers and glared up at Mike.

'What is it this time?' he demanded. 'Thumbscrews? Needles under my nails?' He spoke loudly, so the half-dozen other patients would hear. 'I thought you'd be back. Putting me in hospital isn't enough, is it?'

'Drop the martyr act,' Mike said. 'You put yourself in here. They're all bound to know it.'

Carpenter looked at the pad lying across his knees.

'What's this for?'

'I want you to make a drawing.'

'Of what?'

'The fish pendant you told me Jishrah Gopal wore and carried his dope in. I want you to draw it from memory.'

Carpenter chewed gently at the inside of his cheek, considering.

'What do you want me to do that for? So you can stand up in a court and wave the picture and say it's one more bit of proof against me?'

'How could it ever be that?'

142

'Because you'd twist it to make it any fucking thing you wanted.'

'I want the drawing because it could help in identifying a pendant we've found. I want to know if it's at least *likely* to be the one Gopal owned.' Mike took out a 2B drawing pencil. 'Here. Take your time. Try to set it down as near to your memory of it as possible.'

'I can't draw.'

'Yes you can. We found lots of your drawings. The sketches of Hitler and Himmler. Buckingham Palace with the Nazi flag flying. The crucified negroes. The self-portraits, including the one where you're hung like a donkey. You signed them all, Ross. You're a dab hand with a pencil.'

Carpenter stared at the cover of the drawing pad.

'Why not just show me the pendant you've got — I'll tell you whether it's the one or not. I'm good at remembering detail.'

'What help would that be? You'd say anything at all if you thought it might help your case. We need to check your recollection against what we've got.' Mike bent a little closer. 'If your picture comes near, things could look a lot rosier for you.'

'Bollocks.' It was half-hearted. Carpenter looked up. 'How could it help me, for Christ's sake?'

'It would get our investigation moving in a different direction.'

It wasn't necessarily true. DCS Bingham had already posited the suspicion that Cora Oswyn got the pendant from Carpenter, although so far Cora would say nothing about how she came by it. Mike didn't believe it had come from Carpenter — if it had, he would never have mentioned it in the first place. But the chief did not think along such prosaically commonsense lines; he was capable of believing that in the work of criminal investigation, logic and facts could obscure the truth.

'It'd take me ages,' Carpenter said, acting tetchy to mask his compliance.

Mike held out the pencil again.

'You've all the time you need.'

Carpenter took the pencil and flipped open the drawing pad. He smoothed the top sheet.

'Come back in an hour,' he said.

'Fair enough.'

Mike nodded to the guard, who opened the door and let him leave.

He drove the six miles back to the station and went directly to DCS Bingham's office. Bingham was standing beside his littered desk, talking on the telephone. He nodded as Mike entered. To the telephone he said:

'The man treats his listeners like they're retarded. I don't want him anywhere near me or my men. It's not just his attitude. He upsets people with that elderly smell of his — it's like a mouldy cottage.'

The person at the other end spoke. Bingham stared out of the window.

'No,' he snapped. 'Under no circumstances. I'd sooner have a seminar on the Book of Mormon — it'd be marginally less vacuous. Do it as politely or impolitely as you see fit, but get it across to his people that I can't respect a man whose briefcase possesses more charm than he does.'

The other voice said something in parting. Bingham nodded twice.

'Not at all. Goodbye.'

He put down the receiver and made a face.

'Professor Huckman is touting his criminology lectures round the constabularies. The old bugger's been nothing but a pest since he retired.' Bingham cocked his head enquiringly at Mike. 'What joy, if any?'

'Carpenter's making the drawing.'

'Did you learn anything about the source of the pendant?'

'I showed a picture to one of the lecturers in the Asian Studies department at the university. He's seen things like it before — says they're fairly common. The lettering is modern North Indian Gumukhi script. It's not words, the letters form a hortatory charm. It beseeches fortune to guard the wearer.'

144

'The charm doesn't work then, does it?'

'Not if that's Gopal's pendant.'

'Do you think it is?'

'I'm nearly sure. The cannabis inside might have been a clincher if it had matched the stuff we found in Carpenter's flat.'

'Wasn't it even close?'

'We don't know. A few drops of cannabis oil were kept in the pendant. The owner obviously liked to mix it with the resin. The oil's played hell with the identity of the chunk we found.'

'Sod's law is as constant as gravity.' Bingham tented his fingers under his chin. 'How long till we get the drawing?'

'Forty-five minutes or so.'

'And in the meantime, what measures are being taken with the Oswyn woman? Is she still refusing to co-operate?'

'She's a toughie. Clammed right up, in the end. I think most of it's fright — she doesn't want to talk in case she drops herself in something.'

'I don't suppose she's a possible suspect?'

'About as likely as I am. She's a big harmless tart.'

'I can dream, can't I? What are you doing about her silence?'

'When she finally went shtoom I decided to tell her she's involved in a murder investigation. She said nothing, but her eyes bulged a bit. I sent her home then. Told her we'd be in touch.'

'Good. How long ago was that?'

'About an hour.'

'So, if she's halfway human she'll be some distance up the twist by now. I presume there's no chance of her skipping?'

'I posted a plainclothes WPC in a car outside her place. Chinnery's doing surveillance from a Telecom tent at the back, in case there are any interesting visitors.'

'Good. Fine.' Bingham picked up his telephone again and poised a finger over the keypad. 'Let's pray we're on to something.' He punched in a nunber and pushed the receiver tight against his ear. 'Say goodbye now, Michael. I don't want you to hear the paraphrased version of your bulletin I'm about to improve for the Chief Constable.'

145

Back out in the car park Mike checked his watch and decided there was time to drive over to Melville Court. He took a long route, arriving by a side road and parking fifty yards from the complex of flats. He walked across the common ground at the rear and up to the corner where a striped tent was erected. He pushed his way in through the flap, startling Chinnery, who had been watching Cora Oswyn's windows through binoculars.

'Is she still there?'

'Yes, sir. I think she's drinking. I've seen her at the fridge a couple of times getting ice.'

'Well, in my experience drink doesn't relax anxious women, it makes them jumpy. All to the good, as long as she doesn't overdo it and go *non compos mentis* on us.'

'Is Carpenter co-operating?'

'He seems to be. I'll know soon.'

Mike took the binoculars from Chinnery. He adjusted the eyepieces and propped his elbows on the strut under the opening in the tent wall.

'There's something I meant to ask you,' he said, keeping his eyes to the binoculars. 'Where exactly did you see Cora Oswyn yesterday?'

Chinnery's hesitation was only slight, a missed beat.

'At the club, sir. Revels.'

Mike continued to stare through the binoculars.

'You went there in spite of being ordered not to.'

'I'm afraid I did.'

'Couldn't stop yourself, was that it?'

'I suppose so.' Chinnery cleared his throat. 'Yes, that was it exactly. I was . . . agitated. Badly upset.'

'Cunt struck.'

'It did some good, I think. Going there, I mean. I got my head straightened out.'

'That would have happened without you wading back into the mud.' Mike turned from the binoculars and looked at Chinnery. 'Still,' he said, 'it's done. If you hadn't gone we wouldn't have this lead. *If* it's a lead.' He stepped aside,

146

indicating that Chinnery should take the binoculars again. 'I've no remarks to make on the moral considerations of what you were into, so don't hold your breath on that account.'

'Thank you, sir.'

'There *is* the clinical aspect, though. Without speculating on the hygiene status of the woman you've been involved with, I have to remind you that even the sincerest affection is no safeguard against the ravages of STDs. Tender love has more than one meaning. Get yourself checked, won't you? For your wife's sake as much as your own.'

Chinnery mumbled something.

'Criminal Records have come up with a batch of stuff on Cora,' Mike said, moving on. 'It's all minor, but there's enough to shake her up and make her feel she's under the spotlight.'

'Will you question her on your own next time?'

'I think that would be best. One-to-one's better for inducing the hemmed-in feeling. Besides, if I break the rules, I don't want anyone else's conscience stinging by association.'

Chinnery smiled as Mike let himself out of the tent.

The drawing went beyond anything Mike had hoped for. Carpenter had not only drawn the pendant accurately and in three dimensions, he had included two details — a sharp little indentation on the side, the size of a pencil point, and a twist in the metal loop where the chain passed through — that confirmed it as the one the police now had in their possession.

'You've done a great job,' Mike told him.

'How could I do less for a chum?' Carpenter was still in the chair, still glowering. 'Is it a match?'

'Definitely.'

'What happens now?'

'Like I said, the investigation moves in a new direction.'

'And leaves me where?'

Mike closed the drawing pad and slipped it under his arm.

'You'll be tried under the Drug Trafficking Offences Act,

and I think they might swing the Misuse of Drugs Act at you as well.'

'What about all this murder shit?'

'I don't think you'll be troubled further in that area.'

Carpenter sat nodding slowly.

'So you and Bingham had your fun with me, you threatened me and scared me till all I wanted to do was put my own fucking lights out, and now you're telling me, all calm and casual, that I'm not in the frame any more. You just move on and leave the mess you made. That's what it adds up to, doesn't it?'

Mike looked pensive for a moment.

'Yes,' he said, 'that's what it adds up to. We were insensitive enough to treat you the same way you'd deal with blacks every day of your life, if you got the chance.' Mike nodded for the guard to open the door. 'Thanks again for the drawing.'

'Go and fuck yourself,' Carpenter said.

TWENTY-TWO

Cora Oswyn was not drunk. Five or six whiskies had fused with her anxiety and produced a state of griping apprehension. Her wits were razor sharp. The only clue to the drinking was on her breath.

'I'm sorry I have to trouble you again, Cora,' Mike said. 'It's all right to call you Cora, is it?'

She nodded, three rapid jolts of her head. She sat deep in the thick upholstery, her hands holding each other tightly in her lap, elbows digging in at the junction of the chair's arms and back. Mike sat opposite, leaning forward.

'It's about the pendant, of course. We've got a positive identification. It was the property of a man called Jishrah Gopal. Did you know him?'

'Never heard the name in my life.'

'It was in the papers about him. He was one of the two Asian men who were murdered. The pendant belonged to him. He was wearing it the last time he was seen alive.'

'I didn't know him.' Cora's voice was unsteady. 'That pendant can't have been his, any road. I've had it ages. Yonks.'

'How long, roughly?'

'A year or so. Maybe two years, it's been so long I've forgotten.'

'That just can't be, Cora.' Mike said it with a pained look. 'There's no doubt — none at all — that a very short time ago the very same pendant was hanging round Mr Gopal's neck.'

Cora waggled her head, an effort at indignation.

'You can call me a liar if you like. The truth's the truth, I can't make it different.'

'Don't get agitated, Cora. Just look at the situation the way I have to. You've got a piece of jewellery that belonged to a man who's been murdered. You can't explain, or you *won't* explain, where you got it. You tell us it was a gift, but you can't remember the name of the person who gave it to you. Now, I happen to know you can't have had the pendant long, so you have to be lying about that. You say you never heard of the dead man, yet the pendant was probably round his neck at the moment he died.'

Mike got to his feet. He stood bent over in front of Cora, almost squatting, his hands propped on his knees. He stared into her face.

'Did you kill Jishrah Gopal?'

She squealed and slapped a hand over her mouth. Her eyes above her fingers were wide and scared. When she took her hand away she tried to talk through lips that wouldn't stop trembling.

'Did you, Cora? Was he one of your clients who went too far? Is that it? He hurt you and you lost your temper, or maybe you got frightened, and before you knew it you'd bashed his head in.'

'No! *No!*' She began sobbing, one hand flat on her chest, the other shielding her eyes. 'I never saw him! I wasn't near him! You've got to believe me . . .'

Mike sat down again. He waited for the crying to subside. When she looked at him again her eye make-up had run in blue and black streamers down her cheeks.

'Listen to me carefully,' Mike said. 'We know a lot about you. Our people have put together a dossier that wouldn't win you any medals for honesty, let alone decency.'

'None of it makes me a murderer!'

'You've been charged four times with soliciting and convicted twice. You've two prosecutions for shoplifting and one for theft from a house where you worked as a domestic. You were warned off for loitering a year ago, and it's only eight months since you copped a council reminder that it's a misdemeanour at law to keep a disorderly house.' Mike looked round him. 'It's a nice tidy little flat, Cora. But it's a bit like you. It's deceptive. Misleading. A sham.'

She was staring at him, breathing through her mouth, trembling. He judged it was time to throw on the final straw.

'You won't tell me where you got the pendant,' he said, 'which means you're the only suspect I have. I've no choice but to take you to the station and charge you with the murders of Jishrah Gopal and Ahmed Faiz.'

Cora's eyes looked too big for their sockets. She swallowed, nearly choked.

'I pinched it!' she gasped. 'I was scared to tell you. I saw it on a table in a place I was at. I just picked it up and pocketed it.'

'What place, exactly? *Whose* place?'

'South side, I don't know the name of the street, but I could show you. The guy was a — client. A one-timer. I don't remember his name.'

Mike looked at her and saw no veil of deception, no desperation beyond the simple need to explain. She was telling the truth.

'When was this?'

'Last week.'

'How come you were scared to tell me before?' A show of doubt was important. 'Why keep quiet about a theft when the alternative is to get yourself booked on a murder charge?'

'I've been in a state about it all afternoon.' Cora took a tremulous breath, closing her eyes for a moment. 'At the police station, when you told me the questions were in connection with a murder, my head went into a loop. I wanted to tell you then, I didn't want anything to do with any murder case, but . . .'

Mike waited.

'The pendant, see — it wasn't the only thing I lifted at that place. There was a gold-plated lighter. And money.'

'How much?'

'A hundred-odd quid. I took it out of his pocket when he was in the bog.'

'It still only adds up to theft. Murder's a different league, for heaven's sake. Why did you stay quiet right up until I threatened to charge you?'

'Because — ' Cora made a movement with her hands, like someone balling wool. 'Because there's this thing I've got, my one big terror. Prison. The last time I was up on a thieving charge I got put on weekend remand. I'd never been inside before. Two days, that's all, but it scared me worse than anything ever. I thought I'd go mad.'

'Loss of freedom's a shock.'

'That and the rest of it. The horrible atmosphere. The zombies and dykes and the pukey food. I'll tell you this — freezing on the streets with no place to live, eating out of bins at the back of restaurants — that's got to be better than being a prisoner. I'd die of depression if I went inside.'

'Are you saying you were scared you might go to prison if you coughed to the theft of the pendant?'

'Right. I'd be due to get sent down, what with my previous and the amount I nicked this time. When you said it was a murder investigation I nearly fainted — but still at the back of my mind was prison, prison for sure if I told you how I got the pendant. So I kept telling myself I can't *possibly* get done for some crime I didn't commit.'

'I see,' Mike said.

'The way I reckoned it, it wouldn't work, because they'd need more evidence than a poxy pendant and there wouldn't be any other evidence, not against me, for I didn't do it.'

'You can slow down, Cora. I've caught on.'

'The trouble is,' she went on breathlessly, 'I couldn't convince myself, not all the time, that I *wouldn't* get done for murder — I mean, we've all heard about people being put inside on serious charges and not getting out until years later, and only when somebody discovers there's been a cock up.'

152

'I think you should have a drink, Cora.'

She stared for a moment, taking in what Mike had said. She nodded.

'Yeah, you're right.'

She pushed herself out of the chair and went to the sideboard.

'Fancy one?' she said, holding up a half full bottle of Johnnie Walker.

'No thanks.'

She poured herself a big measure and came back to the chair.

'Aren't you having ice?'

She looked at him curiously.

'How do you know I take ice?'

'I'm a smart arse.'

Cora sat down.

'The ice ran out,' she said.

As she drank she watched Mike. She coughed when the whisky hit her throat, but she didn't lose any.

'Listen,' she said, breathing carefully through her mouth. 'Tell me honestly, will you? Will I get charged for stealing the pendant and the other things?'

'Not if a complaint hasn't been laid, and I doubt one has. And not if you don't go blabbing you took the stuff. We'll keep the pendant, though. And I'll expect a lot of co-operation from you.'

'You can have all you want,' Cora beamed, dropping back in the chair and gulping down most of her drink. 'God, the relief . . . '

'You say you lifted the pendant at the home of a customer. You don't know his name, but you know the place.'

'I was taken there and brought back in a car with the back windows blacked out. That's not as unusual as you might think — some mini-cab companies lay it on for guys that don't want the girls to know where they're going. I recognised the laundry across the road while the driver was hustling me into the place, so I know where it is, all right.'

'Can you show me? Right now, this afternoon?'

'No problem. I'll tell you something, I can't get that guy's face out of my head. I've kept thinking, Christ, I was with a man who's maybe a murderer. Do you think he is, Inspector?'

'He had the pendant in his possession, so he's got some awkward questions to answer. We'll know more when we get down there.'

Mike stood up.

'You won't have to show yourself,' he promised, 'there'll be no risk.'

'There's no risk anyway. When I go on jobs I wear a curly black wig and Madonna make-up. My own mum wouldn't recognise me.'

The switchboard put through a call to Jim Chinnery an instant before the coffee cup reached his mouth. He put it down and snatched up the telephone. The voice at the other end was hoarse and faint.

'I've got something for you,' it said.

'Who am I talking to?'

'A friend.'

'I don't have any friends that sound like you.'

'I'm a new friend. An old enemy of Buster Craig.'

'Any enemy of Craig's is a friend of mine,' Chinnery said. 'What have you got?'

'There's a scam on his new building development, the one on the old Monkswood Hospital site.'

'What kind of scam?'

'He's putting in sub-standard drainage gear and charging for grade A stuff. I can show you the phoney paperwork, the place where the boxes get emptied and re-packed with the duff tackle, the outlet where the good gear gets sold — I can show you the lot.'

'For a new friend you're very generous. How can I take advantage of your offer?'

'Meet me later. The corner of Halcombe Street and Dixon Mews. Know it?'

'East side, right? I'll find it.'

'Six o'clock?'

'No problem. How will I know you?'

'I know you, I'll make myself known.'

'Fair enough.'

'See you later, then.'

'Cheers.'

Chinnery put down the receiver, trying to misinterpret his relief for the sake of his conscience. Before the call he had promised himself, under pressure, that he would call his wife and suggest dinner somewhere. It was not a thing he wanted to do, but he knew he should. He had tried to see it as a double-edged device, doing as much to help along the process of his own recovery as to pump blood through the moribund heart of his marriage.

Now he didn't have to go through with it. Work came first. There was a chance to nail Buster Craig, a villain as good at evading the law as he was at hatching bent ventures. A collar there would go some way to rehabilitating his stature with DI Fletcher, as well as with himself.

He picked up the cup of lukewarm coffee, gulped some, and made a new promise: he would take flowers home to Susie tonight. He hadn't bought her flowers for a long time. Years, probably. He swallowed more coffee, averted a heart-tearing image of Dorothy Beattie and reminded himself, sternly, that he despised her.

TWENTY-THREE

As they headed south in the car Mike asked if Cora hadn't been afraid of a comeback from the client she robbed.

'If he was able to contact you or an intermediary to obtain your services, he could use the same method to make a complaint.'

'He did complain,' Cora said.

Mike glanced at her. She was looking out the window seemingly prepared to leave it at that.

'So? What happened?'

'Well, there's this procedure, see. I always have to tell the switchboard service if I have trouble with a client. If he calls them after that, he gets the bum's rush. After I nicked the pendant and the lighter and the cash, I rang in and said I'd had a hell of a time of it with this punter. I said he roughed me up then threatened to report me for stealing if I didn't give him a freebie.'

'So when he complained he was told to push off.'

'With a warning about the future of his kneecaps,' Cora said, grinning.

'Had you no conscience about that? Not even a little bit?'

She shook her head.

'He was a pig. An animal.' She made a shiver. 'Now I can just imagine him killing somebody. For fun. I'd never regret nicking anything off a guy like that.'

'I must say,' Mike murmured, 'you've an odd lifestyle for somebody with a prison phobia.'

'I can't help myself stealing, sometimes. But after the spell on remand I started playing it safe. I took the trouble to cover myself, always, and I didn't freelance any more. I joined a firm.'

'Jerry Grice's firm?'

Cora looked down at her hands, then out the window again.

'I don't want to talk about the firm.'

'Nothing will get back to them. Anyway, it's part of the co-operation deal.' Mike heard her sigh. 'Tell me how Grice's set-up works.'

She took a minute to answer.

'Officially I'm employed by him part-time as a hostess at Revels. But he makes all the arrangements for my business, too. My real business.'

'You're not the only one on his books?'

'No.'

'How many girls are there, would you say?'

'Seven or eight. It varies.'

'And how does the business work?'

Silence again.

'I've promised, Cora. He won't know you told me.'

'It's straightforward,' she said, sighing again. 'He puts a phone number in certain magazines. It's a separate line he has at the club. All the deals are done that way.'

'What's his cut?'

'Half.'

'Steep.'

'It's worth it. We get protection and regular jobs — a lot of clients pay above the going rate.'

'Which ones pay best?'

'Arabs. They pay top whack. But you bloody earn it.'

Cora directed Mike briskly as they wove down into the network of crisscrossing streets in the south of the city. She kept him clear of congested sectors and one-way systems. This had been her working district years ago, she told him, and she knew nearly every twist and turn.

At an intersection under one of the railway bridges she pointed down a long narrow street.

'Just there,' she said. 'The tall reddish-looking old block on the next corner.'

Mike drove slowly and pulled up opposite the pitted sandstone tenement. Flaked gold lettering on the glass transom said FLEETWOOD MANSIONS.

'The outside's deceptive,' Cora said. 'Inside it's really posh. I was in the left-hand flat on the ground floor.' She turned to Mike. 'What now?'

'We'll sit here for a while and just watch.'

Mike unhooked the radio handset and called the station. He passed on his location and requested a three-man backup.

'Make sure one of them is DC Crampton and tell him to bring his kit.'

Before signing off he asked that DCS Bingham be advised of his movements.

Within ten minutes three plainclothes officers had made radio contact and confirmed they were in position. One was fiddling with the engine of his car, which had shuddered impressively and stopped five yards along the road from Mike. Number two, DC Crampton, was in blue overalls, kneeling in the gutter opposite, poking in a drain with a steel prod. The third man had opted for classical cover: he was leaning on the corner reading a newspaper.

'We'll watch the building another ten minutes,' Mike said, 'then one by one we'll nose our way inside.' He sat back in his seat and folded his arms. 'There's time for you to tell me a few things about the drug scene at Revels, Cora.'

She gave him a hard, wary look.

'I've nothing to do with that. I swear it. I've been mixed up in some hairy things in my time, but never drugs.'

'You must have some idea what goes on, though. You went out with Carpenter a few times, didn't you? He's a pedlar.'

'Twice. I went out with him twice. There's things I don't do, so we agreed there was no point seeing each other after that.'

'But you *have* learned one or two things about the drug dealing at the club?'

'Well, yeah, sort of. I keep my eyes and ears open. It's pretty heavy stuff.'

'Carpenter and Grice, right?'

Cora chewed her lip. She shrugged.

'The promise stands,' Mike said.

'As far as I know,' she said, 'it's mostly Carpenter doing the pushing, but I think Grice is his supplier.' She scratched her head irritably. 'I don't know why I should be telling you all this.'

'Because you're grateful I let you off the hook. And because in spite of the business arrangement, you know Grice is a slime who should be put away. And your natural impulse is to help me because deep down you're a decent soul.'

'*Bloody* deep down.' Cora laughed, then abruptly she jerked forward, pointing. 'That's him!' she hissed.

'Who?'

'The one I lifted the pendant off!'

Mike saw a silver-haired man, tall and athletic looking. He walked smartly through the main entrance of Fleetwood Mansions.

'It's *definitely* him,' Cora said. 'I'd know the dirty sod anywhere.'

'Sit tight,' Mike said.

He got out of the car and crossed the road. DC Crampton withdrew the prod from the drain and stood up slowly, not looking at Mike. The man at the car put down the bonnet, looked about him uncertainly like a stranded motorist, then crossed the road. The officer on the corner closed his newspaper and put it in his jacket pocket. He stayed where he was, leaning, arms folded, watching the doors of Fleetwood Mansions.

Mike entered and went straight to the flat on the left. The door was tall and heavy-looking with an old-fashioned porcelain handle and a brass letter flap. He knocked sharply. DC Crampton came in through the main doors. He moved to the corner at the left and stood there. A moment later the second officer came in; he went to the stairs and climbed to the first landing.

Mike knocked again and waited. He rattled the letter flap and waited again. When there was no response he got down on his knees and looked through the flap. On the floor he could see a couple of advertising news-sheets and scattered circulars. He stood up, beckoning Crampton.

'The gent I want to talk to came into the building a minute ago, but I don't think he's in this apartment. Have you got your toys?'

Crampton took a canvas roll from inside his overalls and put it on the floor. He looked at the lock, grasped the handle and rattled the door gently.

'Nothing fancy,' he said.

He stooped and opened the roll halfway. There were pockets of varying width, each accommodating one or two tools. Crampton withdrew an object that looked like a small pistol with a narrow, blunt-ended probe in place of the barrel. He put the end carefully into the lock and squeezed the trigger twice. He put his ear against the door and listened as he squeezed the trigger a third time, then stood back and twisted the entire tool to the right. The door opened.

'Much obliged.'

Mike went in. There was a short hallway at right angles to the front door, two doors to the left and a single door at the end. The first door on the left was locked. The twin locks looked formidable.

'Can you handle that, Crampton?'

Crampton came in and had a look.

'It'll take a minute or two, sir.'

Mike tried the next door on the left. It opened. Faint daylight filtered through heavy curtains on to a scatter of tea chests and a low table with a typewriter. The floor was uncarpeted. Mike moved on and tried the door at the end of the hallway. It opened. The curtains here were heavier than in the other room and hardly any light came in. He felt along the wall and found a switch. When the soft overhead light went on he whistled.

The room must have cost a fortune to furnish. The carpet was a rich simulated Aubusson, its design matched in paler colours on the textured wallpaper. The curtains were deep plum velvet. There was a Rutton couch and three low-slung Lambert easy chairs. Plain, elegant side tables — one mahogany, the other brass-inlaid rosewood — stood dead-centre on opposite walls. Over the Adam-style fireplace was a gilt-framed oil painting of a Paris street market.

A door in the corner let into a bedroom with a brass four-poster bed, a free standing armoire and a sandalwood dressing table. Beyond that was a bathroom with a recessed bath and a vanitory cupboard, painted throughout in three or four shades of green.

Mike went back to the sitting room. He looked around carefully this time. The room was almost excessively tidy. There were none of the usual traces of occupancy. He spotted a small knee-high bookcase in the corner to the right of the hallway. He examined the spines of the ten or eleven books. They were mostly light novels, but one lying on its side and slipped on top of the others rang a bell straight away: *A Fascist Manifesto for the Nineties*, by John G. Tasker.

Mike went to the hall. DC Crampton was still working on the locked door. In the uncarpeted room Mike opened the curtains. He found a scrap of paper and rolled it on to the platen of the typewriter. Putting his handkerchief over his fingertip, he typed QWERTYUIOP and did it again in lower case. Both times the letter T was clearly misaligned, precisely as it was on the anti-Asian letters.

'Got it, sir,' Crampton called.

Mike went to the hall again. The double-locked door was open a fraction. This room was as heavily curtained as the sitting room. Nothing inside was visible. The two men felt along the walls for a switch. Mike found it.

The light revealed a stark white cube of a room. There was no carpet, but the floor was covered in heavy-duty polythene sheet. There was a stout trestle table on which lay a chisel, a kitchen knife, a hammer and a long jemmy. Behind the door was a two-wheel truck of the type used in bars to move barrels and crates. In the corner, humming softly, was a large commercial freezer chest.

Mike went forward and raised the lid. He started as an interior light came on, an instant after the lid was up.

'Oh, Christ.'

Snowy ice glinted on the silvered interior of the freezer. On the bottom, with a fine glaze and the curiously absent look conferred by death, lay the half-clad body of a young Asian woman, her dark hair spread in a stiff fan around her head. She had bloodied sockets where her eyes had been and a cord was tied tightly round her neck. Her legs were mangled and broken at the knees and bizarrely folded up at her sides.

'Bloody hell, guv . . . '

Crampton watched as Mike reached in and lifted a polythene sandwich bag off the body. He inspected it carefully and saw it contained the girl's eyes.

'What's this?' a voice demanded. 'Who the hell are you?'

They turned and saw the man Cora had pointed out. He stood in the doorway, arms folded, scowling.

'We're the police,' Mike said as the officer from the first landing came into the hallway. 'We've just entered these premises illegally and made an unwarranted search.' He stared at the man, knowing suddenly this wasn't as right and rounded as he wanted it to be. 'I'm glad you showed up. You've saved us the trouble of hunting for you.'

TWENTY-FOUR

His name was Jonathan Gower. His library card and his driving licence confirmed it. He sat now in an interview room at the police station. Three miles away, forensic technicians and policemen submitted the apartment at Fleetwood Mansions to a battery of searches and tests necessary upon the discovery of a suspicious death.

Gower's anger at finding strangers in the apartment had shrunk to mute shock when he saw what Mike had found. In the ensuing minutes he began to look so ill that Mike alerted Dr Armour, the divisional medical officer, who examined Gower as soon as he arrived at the station.

The shock, according to Armour, was authentic and clinically measurable.

'It's the real McCoy,' he told Mike in the corridor outside the interview room. 'He's lethargic and slightly confused. His hands are cold and moist, they're rather blue and so are his lips. The pulse is weak and rapid. He told me he takes tablets for angina. So, for my money he's got mild cardiogenic shock. He'll be all right once he's drunk the sweet tea, but give him time to re-orientate before you put any pressure on him.'

DCS Bingham touched Mike's shoulder as the doctor moved away.

'I've heard some of what's happened,' he said. 'Tell me it all, in shorthand.'

Mike explained about Cora and the pendant, the search of the apartment, the discovery of the third body and the intervention of Jonathan Gower.

'And has Oswyn confirmed he's the man she was with at the apartment?'

'Yes, she has.'

'Do we have the murderer, then?'

'I don't think so.'

'Oh, for God's sake . . .'

'Gower took one look at the body and went into shock. It was definitely a surprise to him. Even before that he didn't look right for the part. His indignation when he found us there — it was unadulterated, if you know what I mean.'

'And I suppose he doesn't know who the dead woman was.'

'He wouldn't take a second look. We don't know who she is either, but the wheels are in motion. Dr Garrett believes she's between twenty and twenty-three years old. She's had at least one child. Her prints and description are circulating, we're getting a photograph made up with closed eyelids inserted, and thirty uniformed men are doing house-to-house in the Asian districts, checking for missing girls.'

'So what do we know about this apartment?'

'Not a lot, until I question Gower.' Mike repeated what the doctor had said about the shock. 'I'll give him a few more minutes, then we'll get started.'

'Talk to me as soon as you know more.'

Bingham went back to his office and Mike slipped along to the toilets. He took off his jacket and tie and washed his face in cold water. He buffed himself dry with a hand towel and when he lowered it Jim Chinnery was standing beside him.

'I've just heard, sir. Is there anything you want me to do?'

'Nothing for the moment.' Mike put on his tie again and combed his hair, making hardly any difference to the random way it lay on his head. 'I might have more idea how to proceed after I've talked to the man we brought in.'

He put on his jacket and they went out to the corridor.

'I've got a meet later,' Chinnery said, not able to keep quiet about it, even though that was what he had planned. 'Somebody says he's willing to finger Buster Craig.'

164

Mike was impressed.

'Sounds like an appointment worth keeping.'

'I'll tell you how it goes.'

You bet you will, Mike thought, letting the cocky note pass without comment, since he believed that bursts of arrogance were a healthy sign in a man re-assembling himself.

'Best of luck.'

Five minutes later Mike entered the interview room and sat down opposite Jonathan Gower.

'How do you feel?'

'Shaky. But I'm not so cold now, and my heart's stopped thumping.' Gower pushed aside the empty tea mug. 'That was a terrible experience. I've never seen a dead body before.'

'It wasn't the best one to see for starters.'

Mike watched Gower carefully. He was surprised, in spite of all his experience, that someone so wholesome-looking could do something that would make a seasoned whore describe him as a dirty sod.

'Do you feel up to talking now?'

'Yes, of course.'

Mike hooked his arm over the back of the chair, trying for casualness.

'Tell me first about the apartment,' he said. 'Is it yours?'

'Heavens, no.' Gower jerked an inch higher. 'What made you think that?'

'Where do you live?'

'At Fleetwood Mansions. I have the downstairs staff flat. I'm the caretaker.'

'So who owns the apartment where we found the body?'

'He's a gentleman who doesn't use the place very often. His real home's somewhere else, I don't know where. I hardly ever see him, although sometimes I can tell he's been to the apartment and gone again.'

'What's his name?'

'Mr Sittim. He's an Indian gentleman.' Gower saw Mike react. 'You know him, do you?'

'We're — trying to trace someone of that name.'

'It's hard to imagine him having anything to do with what you found. He's such a . . . well, he's a civilised man. Very well-mannered.'

Mike unslung his arm from the back of the chair, strategically suspending the casualness. He put both hands on the table in front of him, tightly clasped.

'Mr Gower, do you have a key to Sittim's apartment?'

'We don't have keys to any of the dwellings. We — my wife and myself, that is — look after the central boiler, see to the cleaning of the stairways, the hall floor, the external brasses and so forth. The interiors of the apartments are strictly private.'

'So you've never been in Mr Sittim's place when he wasn't there?'

'No. I've never been in there at all, before today.'

Mike held Gower's eyes, wondering for one fleet second if Cora had lied. He decided she hadn't. There was a new tension in those eyes of Gower's.

'Are you certain about that?'

'Of course I am.' Gower wet his lips. 'I couldn't get in when he's not there, could I? Why are you asking me this, anyway?'

'I'm curious,' Mike said.

The tension spread to Gower's neck. He sat perfectly still, his hands loose on his lap, but his face betrayed the stillness of a man with fear brushing his heart.

'There's a woman who knows you,' Mike said. 'She said she visited you in that flat, the one you say you've never been in before.'

'That's nonsense!' Patches of red appeared on Gower's cheeks. 'Who is this woman?'

'Do you really want me to bring her in here?'

Like ice before a blowlamp, Gower's umbrage began to melt at the edges. He went on staring at Mike, keeping his eyes wide and indignant, but now he simply looked frightened.

166

'She's a prostitute, as you well know,' Mike said. 'She was in that apartment with you, and while she was there she stole something.'

Gower looked down at the bony peaks of his knuckles.

'She took money, didn't she, Mr Gower? And other things.'

'I don't know about anything else,' Gower said, his head still down. 'She definitely took money. A hundred and thirty pounds.' He looked up. 'How do you know all this?'

'I had reason to interview the woman. The story of you and the theft emerged in the course of the questioning.' Mike's head dipped a fraction, his eyes staying on Gower's. 'How did you get into the apartment?'

'I've got a key.'

'Tell me about it.'

Gower picked up the mug, remembered it was empty and put it down again.

'The place was unoccupied for a while, six months or so, after the previous owner died. I had a key, so I could let prospective buyers in to look round. About two months after I got the key I realised the apartment was somewhere I could go. To be on my own, I mean, without anybody else knowing where I was.'

'Without your wife knowing, you mean?'

'People need a break from one another.' Gower said it defensively. 'If you knew my wife you'd agree quick enough.'

'So you began taking women to the empty apartment?'

'Not always. As I said, it was somewhere to go. When I needed a break, say. A bit of peace and quiet. And it wasn't empty, the previous tenant had no relatives and he didn't leave a will, so the furniture stayed as part of the property. It was really quite comfortable, and a lot bigger than my own place.'

'So you must have been annoyed when Sittim finally bought the apartment.'

'I was sorry to hear it was going. But when I met Mr Sittim he told me he would only be using the apartment as a place to get away to occasionally, and only ever at weekends. It was to be somewhere he could take the pressure off.'

167

'Just as it had been for you.'

Gower sniffed.

'When he told me that, I decided I'd get a duplicate key made, before I had to hand over the original.'

'And you've been using the apartment ever since.'

'On and off, yes. But I never abused it. I always left the place exactly the way I found it.' Gower's face seemed to collapse suddenly. His left hand rubbed agitatedly at his right cheek. 'Inspector — I know I must be in some kind of trouble for what I've done . . .'

'Only with Mr Sittim, and only if he finds out. I won't be telling him. I'll be too busy asking him pressing questions — assuming I ever get the chance.'

Gower's fingertips moved to his chin and fussed at the stubble.

'So my wife doesn't need to know?'

'If she's got even average intuition, she'll know at least some of it already.' Mike stood up. 'I want to ask you more questions, Mr Gower, and get a few notes down. But first I'll pop to the canteen and get us some tea. Do you still feel all right?'

'Not bad, considering.'

'Fine. Hold tight. I'll be right back.'

In the corridor Mike spotted DC Wicklow, the resident fraud specialist. He hailed him down.

'I want you to go round to Revels as soon as they're open tonight and bring in Jerry Grice for questioning.'

Wicklow looked delighted.

'Got something concrete on him, sir?'

'I'm well on the way.'

'I'd love to have a go at his books.'

'Keep wishing, Wicklow. You never know your luck.'

Before going to the canteen Mike looked in on DCS Bingham and explained why they were looking for a Mr Sittim again.

'He's our man. Things are moving. The way it's shaping, today might go down as the breakthrough date.'

'I knew I was right to buy heather off that gipsy,' Bingham

said, picking up the telephone and tapping in the Chief Constable's number.

On the way to the canteen, Mike got out his notebook and scribbled *CORA OSWYN — CHOCOLATES*.

The corner of Halcombe Street and Dixon Mews was an unlikely spot for a rendezvous. Halcombe Street was narrow and the traffic was uncommonly heavy; it was difficult for a car to stop, even briefly, without causing an obstruction. The entrance to the mews was halfway blocked with a builder's fence and cluttered beyond that with ladders, scaffolding, mixers and dumper trucks, making it difficult to see if anybody was in the mews. After Jim Chinnery had stood on the corner for five minutes, tapping his feet and tasting traffic fumes, he began to wonder if this was a wind-up.

Then he saw a man standing on the narrow path along one side of the mews. He waved. Jim waved back and began walking, feeling the traffic noise like a backdrop. As he got closer he saw the man had a walking stick. Closer still he began to think he knew the face huddled down in the upturned coat collar.

He narrowed his eyes, trying to make the face register. He was sure he knew that stoat-like arrangement of eyes-nose-mouth. At twenty yards it dawned. He was used to seeing the face in artificial light, that was why it had puzzled him: it was Tony Webb, the assistant manager at Revels.

What does this little pillock want?

As Chinnery drew closer Webb hobbled into a doorway.

What's with the walking stick?

Behind him one rumbling note of the traffic rose, climbing towards a whine. Chinnery craned his neck to see where Webb had gone. He heard the engine note grow stronger and felt vibration in the ground. He looked over his shoulder.

'Jesus — '

The car hit him mid-thigh and spun him in the air. He came down on the roof and bounced, hitting the ground with the side

169

of his head and hearing a clear crack in his chest. He lay there, seeing and hearing everything, feeling nothing.

The car stopped ten yards away. Its red lights went out. White ones came on. The engine roared and the car came rushing back at him, its tyres throwing up stones.

TWENTY-FIVE

'Now emergency action *must* be taken,' Mani Chandra said. He smacked the side of his small fist into the palm of his other hand. 'This very day three of us have been openly threatened with death! This person, this *murderer*, has no qualms about pursuing his course, because he is not being deterred.'

DCS Bingham wrinkled his eyes sympathetically. He had come out of his office to speak to Chandra in the corridor, feeling there was less chance of being cornered out here. Now, seeing the attention the man was attracting, Bingham wished he had spoken to him in private.

'I can appreciate how you feel. It must be very unsettling.'

'Unsettling?' Chandra looked amazed. 'The word is hardly adequate, sir. I am no less than nerve-racked. *Distraught.* Whatever action you are taking, it is simply not adequate. I must insist, on behalf of myself and my people, that more be done — and straight away. It must not be a matter for the delays of board or committee.'

'With respect, Mr Chandra— these threats you've had, they were telephoned, after all — '

'Yes. And my name was named, and I was told in no uncertain terms that I would be next. My friends were told the same.'

'Well, there you are, then.' Bingham spread his hands. 'You can't all be next, can you?'

'It was a direct threat, nevertheless.'

'Look, you were attacked on the street, right? Don't you think if this person was really planning to kill you, he'd have done it then?'

Bingham wondered how Chandra would react if he knew they had found another dead Asian. He had no plans to tell him. He could find out from the newspapers.

'I am not an unreasonable man,' Chandra said, scratching delicately at a long scab on his cheek. 'Even so, I have to be adamant and say I will not budge from here until I have your guarantee of protection, direct and visible, for myself and other leading members of the Asian community.'

As Bingham stood wondering how to get the little man out of his hair, Mike Fletcher was in Number Two interview room, winding up his session with Jonathan Gower.

'I'm grateful you've been so co-operative.' Mike closed his case folder and pocketed his pen. 'What I'd like you to do now is spend a few minutes with the police artist. All we want is a rough idea of what Mr Sittim looks like. We've a lot of standard face components on file, it shouldn't take long to get a reasonable simulation.'

Gower looked exhausted. In the past hour he had disclosed more about himself than he had revealed in his entire life before. Confessions about the women, the types he needed and the number of times he used them had led, necessarily, to an explanation — or at least a description — of the compulsions that drove him at such times. All along he had felt it was important to justify himself, and justification inevitably led to more revelation. He felt, now, that there was nothing of substance about his emotional life that Mike Fletcher did not know.

As they stood up to leave Gower pointed to the case folder in Mike's hand.

'Will all that go on file?'

'Only the relevant parts.'

Gower stroked his cheek.

'It must be hard, deciding what's relevant.'

'Don't worry about it. Your name won't go on the finished deposition.'

When Gower had been handed over to the care of the artist Mike went to the CID room and checked his tray for messages. Nothing new had come in. He stood for a minute staring at the scatter of papers on his desk. That was his understanding of this case, he decided. That plethora of bits and snippets, the random spread of speculation and fact. The answer might be there, if he knew how to link the pieces.

Mea maxima culpa . . .

It *was* his fault. The case should have been tied up long ago. His preoccupations, new and not so new, had been a barrier to lucid thinking. Put plainly, as he would have put it to another copper, he was passing off cowshed confetti as detective work, because his hobby-horses kept too much of his attention away from the job.

'See to it, dickhead,' he murmured.

Ten minutes later he walked into the city mortuary. Dr Garrett was in the office, working on an autopsy protocol. He was obviously pleased to be interrupted.

'Come in, Michael. Throw some papers on the floor and sit down. If it's a preview you're after, I can tell you the Asian woman died in exactly the same way, and at the same hands, as the two men.'

'I never doubted it.'

'It *was* something of a foregone conclusion.' Garrett sat back, rubbing his hands. 'Could I tempt you to a dram, at all? I was thinking of having one a minute before you appeared.'

'The power of magical thinking,' Mike said, taking a bottle of Ballantine's from his pocket. 'My treat.'

He twisted the cap and broke the seal. He took the two miniature lab beakers from the filing cabinet, set them on the desk and poured two good measures.

'Health,' he said, handing one to Garrett.

'And the wealth to enjoy it.'

They drank.

'So . . . ' Garrett watched as Mike cleared a chair. 'What is this tasty drop going to cost me?'

Mike sighed softly as he sat down.

'I'd never make a con man.'

'Never,' Garrett agreed. 'There's a searching, wistful quality behind your eyes that gives you away. It's at its strongest when you're looking for a perch to land on. What's the problem?'

'The case. I've got nowhere with it.'

'Oh.' Garrett looked surprised. 'I've been assuming it's headed towards a resolution. Am I wrong?'

'I think we're close,' Mike said. 'But it's all been so bloody . . . amateur. We, or rather *I*, should have cut across the procedure and the lines of enquiry long ago and nailed our villain. I've been unprofessional. It bothers me.'

'I'm sure you'll feel differently when it's all over.'

Mike stared.

'Sorry,' Garrett said at once. 'You've *not* come for the cheap comforting platitudes, I take it.'

'No, I haven't.'

'Tell me, then.'

'I'd still like to solve this mess. I want to crack it before it unfolds automatically under the sheer weight of procedure — with the possible loss of more life in the meantime. I came here because I want the use of a cold eye.'

Garrett twiddled his pen in one hand, raised his glass to his lips with the other. He smiled as he sipped.

'All of me,' he sighed, 'why not take all of me . . . '

'Pardon?'

'You're inclined to use me piecemeal these days. Last time it was my sympathetic ear. Now it's my cold eye. What ever next?' Garrett saw the flash of impatience. 'Sorry again,' he said. 'Do proceed.'

'I get the feeling,' Mike said, 'that I've missed something. It's been there, right in front of me, but I haven't caught on.'

'Well, if we're going to talk in those terms, let's be scientific, shall we?' Garrett put down his glass. 'Start by defining what's missing.'

Mike thought.

'A wrong note,' he said. 'A duff rhyme.'

'An incongruity.'

'Right. There's always one. At least one.'

'Or the opposite, yes? A congruity so tidy, so harmonious, that it just doesn't belong in the real world.'

'A poetic distinction,' Mike said. 'It counts as an incongruity.'

'Of course.' Garrett pointed to the papers on his desk. 'I'm dealing with one such here. The deceased was an absolute pillar — banker, councillor, school governor, anti-abortion campaigner, church sidesman. A solid father and doting grandfather. He stood out among his peers like a unicorn at a bullfight, and put in forty years of public service without so much as a whiff of scandal. Then two days ago they found him hanging over the staircase, naked except for a rubber raincoat, suspended by a dog collar and leash. He had a plastic mask over his face and three rubber bands wound round his penis. Cause of death was masochistic asphyxia.'

Garrett took a delicate sip of whisky. Mike refilled his glass and did the same.

'Conversely,' Garrett went on, 'there was a case a month or two back, I don't know if you remember — Gamage, was it? Some name like that. He was avoiding arrest and ran smack into the front of a moving bus. Traumatic evisceration of the brain. It shot right into the gutter . . .'

'Ramage,' Mike said. 'Male prostitute, blackmailer, pornographer, common thief.'

'He constituted the kind of incongruity that would catch the attention at once,' Garrett said, 'even in a case littered with malefactors. He possessed not one decent bone in his entire loathsome body. He actually looked evil — although the open-top head did a lot to prejudice the effect.' He sighed. 'None of this is much help, is it?'

Mike shrugged.

'You need to go back to basics,' Garrett said. 'It's procedural again, but it's the only advice I can offer. Lay out everything you know on a big blackboard. Then try fitting the pieces into categories of explanation, setting aside the items that don't fit. When you've tried cross-slotting the misfits and have your final residue — '

'It occurs to me,' Mike said, 'that I could have been standing too close to something, or somebody . . .'

'You weren't listening,' Garrett said bleakly. 'I'll need that breath when I'm dying.'

'Have another drink.'

Garrett held out his glass, watching Mike's face as he poured.

'You've picked up a thread, have you?'

'I don't know,' Mike said. 'It's like chasing somebody in the fog. Maybe if we set it down in broad outlines, what we don't know . . . For a start, what kind of man are we looking for? He kills and he mutilates, but he won't mutilate while the victim is alive. So, he wants to kill, but not hurt.'

'He wishes to create an illusion of savagery, and he manages it, more or less, in spite of his qualms.'

'Right,' Mike said.

'That betrays an uncommonly disciplined personality.'

'Why does it?'

'Because anyone less than *rigorously* bound by his purpose would be likely to botch things.' Dr Garrett sniffed his drink. 'It takes an unusually tight and tidy mind to go through with the kind of plan apparent from these murders.'

Mike poised his glass between the fingertips of both hands. He stared at it, a wizard contemplating entrails. In the quiet room the clock ticked comfortingly. Out along the corridor knives rattled on porcelain.

'Jesus Christ,' Mike said.

He swallowed all the whisky in his glass. He put it down and stood up.

'Tidiness,' he said, buttoning his coat, hurrying. 'Congruity. When some bells go off I can't catch the pitch.'

'Eh?'

'Other people suspect appearances more than I do,' Mike said. 'Maybe I shouldn't be a cop at all.'

'You're frothing, old chap.'

'No wonder. I'm such a sucker for innocence — especially the pure and wounded kind. I'm not *chary* enough. Remember the policeman who got beaten up in a city-centre bank raid — two, three years ago? PC Bannister? He turned out to be an accomplice. It never occurred to me, but you tumbled him, and you took the trouble to explain to me how.'

'Self-inflicted wounds,' Garrett said. 'Is that the one?'

'That's the one,' Mike said, heading for the door.

The house stood at the end of a secluded residential terrace, behind a high white wall with a black iron railing along the top. The drawing-room window was shaded by twin flowering cherry trees, standing eight feet apart in the middle of a twenty-foot rectangle of trimmed lawn.

Tidy, Mike thought, pressing the shiny brass bell push.

The door was opened by Mani Chandra. He wore a dark blue silk dressing gown and a yellow cravat. He smiled and managed a tiny frown at the same time.

'Inspector,' he said. 'You've come, I assume, on the matter of security I discussed with your superintendent.'

He stood aside to let Mike enter. Mike stayed where he was, on the step. He stared fixedly at Chandra, at the scratches on his face.

'I want you to come back to the station with me,' he said.

Chandra inclined his head.

'Why, may I ask?'

'I believe you can help us with our enquiries into the recent killings of three Asian people.'

For an instant Chandra looked shocked. Then his face became calm. He began to say something, then stopped himself. He cleared his throat, waving a hand behind him.

'If you would allow me a minute to change, Inspector . . .'

'Of course.' Mike followed him into the hall and closed the door. 'Take all the time you need.'

TWENTY-SIX

They sat at the table in Number One interview room — Mike Fletcher and DCS Bingham on one side, Mani Chandra opposite. For the tape Mike recited the date, the time and the names of those present.

Chandra had come here without resistance. He had admitted, when asked by Mike, that he used the name Sittim and that he owned an apartment in that name at Fleetwood Mansions. He had no objection to being questioned in connection with three murders, and he did not ask for his lawyer to be present. To all appearances he had become entirely passive.

DCS Bingham hardly knew where to begin.

'Maybe we should start by establishing some facts. Mr Chandra, were you involved in the deaths of Jishrah Gopal and Ahmed Faiz?'

'I killed both men,' Chandra said, his eyes wide and candid.

'Detective Inspector Fletcher has found a third body, a young woman this time, at your apartment. I presume you killed her, too?'

Mani Chandra nodded solemnly.

'And the attack on Gordon Beames,' Mike said. 'You did that?'

'Indeed.' Chandra touched a finger to his lips. 'There was a failure of continuity there.' He almost smiled. 'I couldn't bring myself to use a metal hook on him as I had planned. I used the club only. Conversely I couldn't sum up the courage to hit myself with the club, yet I found it relatively easy to make these.' He touched the scratches on his face. 'I used my fingernails.'

Mike didn't need to be told. It stung him that he hadn't realised before.

'What about the threatening letters?' he said. 'Had you anything to do with those?'

'I wrote them. All of them.'

'There's something I have to ask right now,' Bingham said, flicking a glance at Mike. 'After all the trouble you took to cover your trail and bamboozle us, why are you owning up without a fight?'

Now Chandra did smile, though thinly, without warmth.

'A deception should be pursued with vigour, Superintendent. It must be carried out with complete dedication. But if it fails, in spite of all you have done to make it work, then it should be abandoned with as much vigour as it was embraced. Do you follow me?'

'Uh, kind of, I suppose.'

'To sustain a damaged deception,' Chandra went on, waving his hands in tight circles, 'even one that is only semi-discredited, is to injure oneself spiritually. There may be physical consequences, too. It is my philosophy that a good deception can change a man's life radically, as nothing else can, but a *failed* deception can do him nothing but harm — here and hereafter. It is like something decaying that clings to his spirit. He must cast it off, and he does that by confessing it all.'

Mike listened to the confident delivery, watching the animated, intelligent face. Chandra's madness had a disquieting appeal.

'I am frank and direct with you now, gentlemen, because the architraves of my duplicity have cracked. I have no further use for the structure.' He narrowed his eyes and made a sound, a truncated giggle. 'I am, as they once put it, undone, and in many ways it is a relief. The strain at times has been formidable.'

All three were silent for a minute, Chandra gazing at his neatly folded hands on the table, Mike and DCS Bingham scribbling notes and occasionally glancing at each other.

Finally Mike spoke.

'If the Superintendent agrees, Mr Chandra, I think it would save time if you told us your story from the beginning.' Bingham was nodding already, happy to agree. 'It's important you tell us everything — especially *why* you did all these things.'

'I will be happy to explain everything, Inspector.'

It took nearly an hour. Chandra insisted on telling his story in minutest detail. He gave times and places, he explained the circumstances surrounding events and the motives underlying his own reactions. The tale was delivered at speed, as if it were being read off a page, and all the time Chandra waved his hands, conducting his own thoughts.

It had begun in 1967 when Chandra, aged thirty-two, a school teacher from Delhi, came to England with his father to visit relatives in Bradford. Mani had dreamed of visiting Britain since boyhood, and now he was there he liked the country so much he wanted to stay. Under the immigration laws that wasn't possible. So he ran away. For two years he worked at a string of cash-in-hand jobs in London and Bristol, saving his wages and living rough. Eventually the opportunity came to buy into a small canned-food import business. He invested most of his savings and with what remained he bought forged immigration documents and a British passport.

'In those days it was much easier than now,' he said. 'It was cheaper, too, and the quality of the documents was superb.'

For fifteen years he devoted himself to growth. His business ventures expanded, and so did he. He spent his spare time in study, enriching his mind, broadening his grasp of commerce and culture. He became modestly rich and worked at raising his social standing by ingratiating himself with people who could help him up the ladder. By the time he was forty-five in 1980, he was firmly established in the city as a businessman and a leader in the Asian community. For the first time since he came to England, he felt secure.

Then, in 1982, one of his prosperous neighbours was arrested and eventually deported. He had been an illegal immigrant, and somehow the authorities had found out. Mani watched the press carefully after that. He discovered that the uprooting of illegal immigrants all over Britain was being stepped up as a matter of policy. There were even special investigators, men and women trained to track down those who didn't belong.

'That was bad news,' Chandra said. 'I don't know if you can imagine how I felt. I was financially secure, I was respected in the community and accorded honours and privileges to right and left — yet at any minute my secret might be discovered, I could lose everything and be sent back to languish in the benighted place I came from. I tell you candidly, I used to have nightmares.'

In 1985 he had his first — and only — confrontation with the immigration authorities. He was summoned to London and seated before eight men at a long table. They quizzed him for an hour on how he came to be living in England, and demanded evidentiary documents of his commercial progress — in particular, records which could be followed backwards. Mani was able to satisfy their demands, but he was left feeling dangerously overstretched.

Later, consulting a barrister on the matter, Mani was told it simply wasn't enough to have papers nowadays; since documents could be forged, you needed a credible and above all *checkable* story. Fortunately for Mani he had a long and plausible record of commercial achievement in Great Britain. It stemmed — according to a particular false document laid away for a rainy day — from the legitimate business activity of his deceased uncle, a real corpse buried at Barnet whose name just happened to be the same as Mani's.

'I was never the same after the interview with the immigration people. They were so stern with me. So hostile. I could see they would jump at any chance to deport me and I soon forgot what it was like to feel safe.'

Then, five years after the disturbing experience with the authorities, Mani was visited at his home by two men: Jishrah Gopal and Ahmed Faiz.

'They made their mission very plain. They had no reliable

papers, they said, but they knew I had. They also knew, by whatever means, that my papers were forgeries. I would get them papers like mine, they said, and in exchange they would forget all about me.'

Mani came to accept that Jishrah and Ahmed represented a problem on the increase, one that was not likely to go away. He pictured the authorities running closer and tighter checks on everybody in the Asian community, until the day came when his own alibis and pretexts would blow apart.

'Unless we all began to look like victims, I suddenly thought. It was clear — I needed to gain sympathy and concern for me and my kind, and simultaneously get rid of the hazard to my safety. I read the racist literature. I bought a couple of books and composed a few diatribes. I became good at it, don't you think?'

Mike admitted — to himself — that the letters had taken him in. He had been looking for the owner of the tone of voice they reflected. Until now, he would never have believed an Asian could have concocted them.

'In the meantime,' Mani went on, 'I laid my plans for the destruction of the two illegals. There was no question of acceding to their demands — they were drug users, unreliable men, the kind who would be knocking on my door and threatening me whenever the least crisis loomed. There was only one way to be rid of them. So I told them I could put them in touch with Mr Sittim, a gentleman who would furnish them with papers, though they would be expensive. The price defused any tendency they might have had to disbelieve me.'

He arranged a meeting, emphasising the need for strict secrecy. It was at the apartment in Fleetwood Mansions, a place Chandra retreated to at odd times, but which had been bought as a hideaway should he ever find himself in crisis with the authorities.

'The rest you have probably worked out for yourselves. The two men came to the back entrance, the very way by which they left later, at separate times, on a barrel truck. I made their deaths look like racist murders — although I must point out I had no interest in hurting them. To the best of my knowledge they did not suffer.'

Bingham asked about the drug he used.

'It is called haloperidol. I have substantial quantities. They came from a diverted consignment of pharmaceuticals that a crooked ex-employee of mine had the effrontery to hide in my warehouse. I confiscated the drugs and would have destroyed them, until I read the data sheets packed with the haloperidol tablets. The drug appeared to have fascinating properties. I threw away half the consignment and kept the rest.'

After the discovery of the first body, he adopted an act to reinforce the image of himself and other Asians as victims.

'Publicly I behaved like a frightened, outraged patriarch. For an added authentic touch I even put on built-up boots and attacked the English boy — Beames spends time with the daughter of an Asian family I know. Oh, I thought it was all working wonderfully well.'

Mike asked who the girl in the freezer was.

'A prostitute.'

'Was she an illegal alien?'

'I have no idea, Inspector. I killed her to — how do you put it? — muddy the water. It occurred to me, with hindsight, that some pattern might become discernible from the fact that I killed two friends — it occurred to me, also, that it might be possible to determine that they died at the same time — did your forensic people discover that?'

'Yes,' Bingham said, 'they did.'

'I should have spent more time studying forensic science. However, I *did* study enough general criminology over the years to know that patterns in crime — especially in murder — are to be avoided. So I decided to throw in a non-pattern killing and create what I believe is called a — a randomity factor, yes?'

Mike nodded.

'I took the girl to the apartment on the pretext of wishing

183

to have sex. I had plans to dump her body later this month on a roundabout in the Asian children's playground.'

Chandra sat back. His story was finished. He asked if he might have a glass of water. When it came he drank half of it in one go, then he looked at Mike.

'One of my best assets in all this nefarious activity has been my size — my apparent physical delicacy. I simply don't look like a man who could kill a fly without a struggle.'

He put down the glass and asked the officers to take their hands off the table. When they did, he gripped the edge with one hand; his shoulders squared smartly and he set his teeth. He closed his eyes and slowly raised his arm. Impressively, the heavy table came a clear inch away from the floor. Chandra let it down gently and smiled.

'A discipline I learned as a student in India. Mental energy is converted to physical strength whenever necessary. Lugging those bodies about was probably easier for me than it would be for men of your stature.'

He looked at Mike again.

'What did I do wrong? Did that caretaker person get into my apartment? I was sure those locks would deter anybody.'

'It's a long story. What you did wrong was to leave Jishrah Gopal's pendant lying around.'

'Oh dear, dear.' Chandra looked immensely sad. 'I had intended to throw it in the river, but I forgot.' He shrugged. 'There you are. All that fine planning, and one silly oversight ruins everything. That is life, isn't it?'

Mike watched the fastidious, rueful face. He read serious intent. Time seemed to slow down again. Chandra raised the glass to his mouth. An instant before the rim touched his lips the other hand came up, much faster.

Mike threw himself across the table and grabbed Chandra's wrist. He brought the small hand down with a crack on the edge of the table. Chandra howled. His fingers went slack and a capsule fell on the table. When Mike let go Chandra pushed his hand into his armpit and rocked back and forth with the pain.

Bingham grabbed the capsule.

'What's this, Mr Chandra? More haloperidol?'

'Potassium cyanide,' Chandra said, his face solemn. 'Now I am afraid everything really is ruined.'

Later, leaning on the bar in the police club, Bingham felt he had to explain to Mike that it was over. They had won. The killer was in the coop. Whitehall's robotic goons wouldn't be moving in after all. He told Mike to lighten up.

'I'll shake out of it after a couple of drinks,' Mike said. 'It's Chandra. I can't get him out of my head. It's his casualness. The way he accepts murder as a reasonable expedient. He spooked me. Mad folk usually do.'

'He's a nutter all right,' Bingham said. 'A full pork pie short of a picnic. But they'll find him fit to plead. Front seats at *that* trial should fetch a few bob.'

Mike swallowed a whole whisky at once and ordered another. The big barman took the glass to the optic. He addressed Mike and Bingham over his shoulder.

'Does either one of you know the difference between a soldier and a policeman, by any chance?'

They looked at each other, shook their heads.

'Well,' the barman said, 'you can't dip a policeman in your egg.'

In the context of the kind of day it had been, that was extraordinarily funny. Both men burst out laughing. Mirth washed over Mike like cool water. He turned, still laughing, and put his elbows on the bar.

It was then, with the worst timing imaginable, that DS Tommy Lafferty, from Eastern Division CID, came into the bar to tell them Jim Chinnery was dead.

TWENTY-SEVEN

On a murky Friday night with leaden, lopsided clouds hanging low over the city, Mike Fletcher and Kate Barbour had dinner in Douglas's. It was one of the few restaurants in the city specialising in English food. The menu offered such specialities as celery and stilton soup, mackerel and rhubarb, chicken with cream and cider, beefsteak with oyster sauce, grapefruit chiffon pie and baked rum custard with raspberry sauce. The establishment also boasted the widest selection of British cheeses obtainable anywhere. A few times in the past Mike had said he would like to eat at Douglas's, but he resented the unreasonable prices and the restaurant's consequent snob appeal. Tonight he seemed to have no such reservations.

Coming so soon after Jim Chinnery's death, the invitation had surprised Kate. She was not aware, yet, that at times of personal distress Mike could find relief in the distractions of a busy restaurant. On the evening his wife finally left him he took his daughter Moira to dinner. When Moira died he kept himself busy all day arranging the funeral and telephoning relatives; in the evening he went straight from the office to a favourite Italian restaurant, where he kept the lid on his grief for another three hours.

Tonight he had telephoned Kate as soon as the loose ends began to show signs of tidying themselves. The case work had come under control too fast. He still needed distraction.

'I'm no good at demonstrating fury,' he said as they finished their meal. 'But I'm a dab hand at feeling it. Jim's been dead six days and the anger still comes over me in waves. Until the third or fourth glass of wine tonight I was really primed to do murder.'

'It showed,' Kate said. She pushed aside her plate. 'It didn't look like homicidal abstraction, though. More like aggravated constipation.'

Mike wrinkled his nose, pleased she took the trouble to keep the tone from turning maudlin.

'When you were in the Ladies I even fantasised going back to the cells and killing Jerry Grice. With an axe.'

'Did it make you feel better?'

'It didn't make me feel anything. I don't think actually killing the bastard would give me much of a buzz either. That's the curse with some vacuums. Nothing's extreme enough to fill them.'

Kate split the remainder of the wine between their glasses, giving Mike slightly more.

'There's no chance of Grice slipping out from under?'

'Not a hope,' Mike said. 'Proving the case won't call for any fine-tuned expostulation from the prosecution. There were bits of Jim all over Grice's car.'

Two small lines appeared between Kate's eyes as she imagined that.

'You'd have thought,' she said, 'the first thing a criminal would do after a hit and run would be to wash the evidence off the vehicle.'

'He'd have done it, if his luck had been better. When DC Wicklow went to the club to pick Grice up for questioning, he wasn't there. So Wicklow, never a lad to give up, went down to the yard at the back of the club where the garages are. He waited. Not long after, Grice drove in. He and Webb got out of the car. Wicklow noticed the state of the wheels and paintwork, and he saw Grice was heading straight for the hosepipe. So he stepped out of the shadows and told both men to freeze. They did the opposite — they started moving faster. Grice got hold of a brick and came at Wicklow with it. Webb tried to hit him with his walking stick.' Mike broke off and sat back, his head tilted, appraising Kate's open-mouthed attentiveness. 'Racy stuff, isn't it?

'Go on!' she squeaked. 'What happened?'

'Wicklow kicked the feet from Webb, grabbed his stick and crowned Grice with it.'

'Wonderful.'

'I'll say. Gave him another mouth — a six-stitcher.'

Mike toasted Kate perfunctorily with his glass and took a swallow.

'Grice is going on his longest holiday yet. The shit-hot execution of three search warrants got us all the evidence we need on the drug and vice operations. He could get life plus life.'

Kate watched Mike's imitation of grim satisfaction.

'But none of it,' she said, 'will bring back Jim.'

'No.' Mike let sadness take hold for a moment, then he pushed himself up in his seat. 'Tell me, while we're talking shop — what did you make of manic Mani?'

'He's creepy,' Kate said. She had visited Chandra in the remand centre to make a psychiatric evaluation for the Crown. 'He's a schizoaffective type. It would take weeks to map his mental profile with any accuracy. But I'll tell you this — he'll kill himself the first chance he gets. He views the business of losing everything and going to prison as the ultimate inconvenience. He can't see the point of living without the things he likes. For him, going suicidal is just one more practical decision.'

'I should have caught on to him sooner. I was too busy being put-upon by his moral rectitude. Dr Garrett told me how to identify self-inflicted facial wounds years ago. I take it you know all about that, of course.'

Kate nodded.

'They're usually superficial, parallel, and they avoid the sensitive parts like eyes, ears, nose and lips.'

'How long before I retain enough to be a hot shot? My ignorance depresses me.'

'You shouldn't let it get you down,' Kate said soothingly. 'Some people are just born kind of, well, limited. It doesn't make you a bad person.'

Mike grabbed her knee under the table and squeezed. She yelped and splashed wine on the table cloth.

'Prole!' she hissed. 'Savage! Working-class ruffian!'

'Yeah,' he growled, and squeezed again, sliding his hand along her thigh.

'Your place or mine?' she said loudly in her Princess Anne voice.

They laughed, exhilarated by the resurgence of fun. It had been a long time since they had clowned.

'Can we make it your place?' Mike said, his voice more serious now. 'After coffee and brandies, of course.'

'Certainly,' Kate said. 'My place is your place.'

'Not yet.'

'That wasn't the thin edge of a wedge, Mike.'

'I know. But if you *are* tempted to railroad me, you should know there's no need any more.'

'Why is that?'

'I'm on some kind of countdown,' Mike said. 'I'm not in control of it. What happens is, before I go to bed each night I put a few more of my things into suitcases and tea chests.'

It was an endearing fiction, designed to bridge the time until no lie would be needed. Kate, moved by the kindness, reached out and touched Mike's face.